Samuel French Acting Edition

A Turn for the Nurse

by Rick Abbot

I0591874

‖ SAMUEL FRENCH ‖

SAMUELFRENCH.COM   SAMUELFRENCH.CO.UK

FOR PRODUCTION ENQUIRIES

UNITED STATES AND CANADA
Info@SamuelFrench.com
1-866-598-8449

UNITED KINGDOM AND EUROPE
Plays@SamuelFrench.co.uk
020-7255-4302

Each title is subject to availability from Samuel French, depending
upon country of performance. Please be aware that *A TURN FOR
THE NURSE* may not be licensed by Samuel French in your territory.
Professional and amateur producers should contact the nearest Samuel
French office or licensing partner to verify availability.

Please refer to page 115 for further copyright information.

CAST OF CHARACTERS
(In Order of Appearance)

SYLVIA CRANE, an impoverished lady, madly enamored of
DEREK STRATTON, ne'er-do-well nephew of a wealthy
    family
JANE JOHNSON, maid-of-all-work at the Stratton mansion
GEORGE STRATTON, simply splendid son of that wealthy
    family
Ms. J.D. CULVER, the wealthy family's family lawyer
HERBERT SANDERS, the wealthy family's ambitious butler
OLIVER STRATTON, lovelorn patriarch of this wealthy
    family
PEGGY BRENT, his temporary live-in nurse, a health nut
WU CHANG, a somewhat unorthodox recruiter from Tibet
CORA VAN BECK, emissary of an anti-alcohol association

TIME: the present, about mid-September
LOCALE: The Stratton Mansion on Long Island

ACT ONE
Scene 1: a pleasant evening just before dinner
Scene 2: that evening at dinner

ACT TWO
Scene 1: that evening just after dinner
Scene 2: about fifteen minutes later

ACT THREE
approximately five minutes later

For
JANE NiGH DAVIDSON,
basically a beautiful person,
always an able actress, and
someday a superb ''Sylvia''

A Turn for the Nurse

ACT ONE

SCENE 1

Curtain rises on the library of the Stratton mansion on Long Island. Half the Upstage wall is devoted to a pair of floor-to-ceiling bookcases. A door in the Upstage Right wall leads to the front hall. Glass-paned doors in the Upstage wall, Left, lead to a garden. Between the matched bookcases hangs a large painting*; there is a wall safe behind it, visible only when the painting slides upward. Center stage is a long table with a vase of flowers at each end. In the center of the table is a silver tray with ice bucket, soda siphon, liquor, glasses, etc. upon it. Down Left, a desk with swivel chair is against the wall; at the moment, it has a large woman's purse upon it. A number** of chairs are lined here and there against the walls. Before the table, its upper edge at a level with the table surface, is a large sofa. The sofa is occupied by a man and woman. The man and woman are preoccupied by a long kiss. The man is DEREK STRATTON, *the woman is* SYLVIA CRANE. *They are not in love, but fun is fun. As they take a breather, we see that he is young and handsome, and she is young and pretty; they seem to notice this at the same moment, and begin yet another long kiss.* JANE JOHNSON, *the maid, enters from hall.*

*some dreadful artwork
**seven

5

JANE. Master Derek, sir, cook is making individual desserts.

DEREK. Tell her I wish her luck. (*Resumes kissing* SYLVIA.)

JANE. Master Derek, sir, she wants to know how many.

DEREK. Just one, Jane, thank you.

JANE. For the entire family?

DEREK. For me, Jane. I never take more than one dessert. Tell her to make it extra large. (*Resumes again.*)

JANE. I mean, sir, how many will there be for dinner?

DEREK. There will be four, Jane. Uncle Oliver, George, myself and Miss Brent.

JANE. The nurse? But sir—

DEREK. Hold on, better make it five. Ms. Culver is dropping in tonight to take care of the legal end of things. She will undoubtedly join us for dinner.

JANE. (*Indicating* SYLVIA.) And Miss Crane—?

DEREK. Miss Crane is dining alone. At the Automat.

JANE. Cook will be upset.

DEREK. Because Miss Crane is dining at the Automat?

JANE. No, sir. Because that nurse is dining with the family.

DEREK. Even a nurse must eat, Jane.

JANE. But she talks medicine all the time, sir. Remember the time we had that nice tapioca pudding, and she began describing that brain tumor? Nobody finished their dessert.

DEREK. Jane, Miss Brent is a dedicated woman. Medicine is her life. She would naturally discourse upon her favorite topic. (*Beat.*) By the way—we're not *having* tapioca, are we—?

JANE. Cook said never again.

DEREK. Then tell her there will be five for dinner, Jane.

JANE. (*Darkly.*) Cook won't like it! (*Exits to hall.*)

SYLVIA. Derek, darling—

DEREK. You talk too much. (*Resumes kissing her;* GEORGE STRATTON, *another handsome young man about his same age, strolls in from hall.*)

GEORGE. Hello, Derek. Is that Peggy?

DEREK. I never consort with the hired help.

GEORGE. (*Before* DEREK *can quite resume kissing.*) Do you have any notion where she is? I can't find her.

DEREK. Have you tried cutting your throat, George? She's sure to pop up with a band-aid and a lecture on clotting-time.

GEORGE. Oliver wants her, I don't.

SYLVIA. Have you tried cutting *his* throat?

GEORGE. (*Recognizing her.*) Sylvia! Didn't expect to find *you* here. Have you and Oliver buried the hatchet?

SYLVIA. Sorry, George, no. I'm just living dangerously.

GEORGE. Well, you needn't worry much longer. Once the will is probated, you two won't have to do your necking in secret.

SYLVIA. Secret?! We'd have more privacy onstage at a Rock Concert!

GEORGE. Has Oliver come in here yet?

DEREK. He's about the only one who hasn't.

GEORGE. But you haven't seen Peggy? Do you suppose she might have taken a stroll in the garden?

SYLVIA. George, Nurse Peggy Brent is not yet thirty, there is a full moon, and the primroses are bursting from their buds like popcorn.

DEREK. She mean "yes," George. Peggy could very well have passed through here while we were otherwise occupied—her sensible shoes have rubber soles.

GEORGE. (*Starts toward garden.*) Maybe I'll find her under the trellis— (*Exits too quickly to hear:*)

SYLVIA. Or under a rock.

DEREK. Where were we?

SYLVIA. Top of the ninth, tie score. (*They resume kissing;* J.D. CULVER, *a woman in her early sixties, very well dressed, enters from hall, a coat over her arm.*)

J.D. Hello-hello-hello!

DEREK. J.D. Culver, as I live and breathe! How's the slightly graying girl lawyer?

J.D. (*En route to desk.*) Wistful. After all—autumn, a full moon, primroses perfuming the air, nightbirds singing, and now, you two, loving one another on the sofa. It makes me quite lonesome for—Wolfgang.

SYLVIA. (*Touched.*) Your husband?

DEREK. Her schnauzer.

J.D. His little wet nose, soft brown eyes, and that silly little ring.

SYLVIA. He wore a ring?

DEREK. Around one eye, dearest. Wolfgang passed from this world three months ago, in a dispute over a right-of-way.

SYLVIA. Who was disputing with him?

J.D. A milk truck. (*Tosses coat onto desk chair.*)

DEREK. (*Rises.*) I'd better get you out of here, love. Oliver is sure to show up soon.

SYLVIA. (*As they cross to* J.D.) Sorry to rush off like this, but you know how Oliver feels about me. Derek doesn't dare take any chances of him changing his will. (*Laughs lightly as she and* DEREK *start toward garden doors.*)

J.D. I don't think he'd change it again *today*. He seemed pretty sure of himself when he changed it yesterday.

(DEREK *and* SYLVIA *stop dead at the garden doors; still arm in arm, like a film running in reverse, they walk backwards until they have once more come to face* J.D. *before desk.*)

DEREK. (*Voice cracking.*) Changed?

SYLVIA. (*Similarly.*) The will?

BOTH. Yesterday?

J.D. You didn't know? Oh, well, you'll hear about it soon enough, I guess. (*Turns away toward desk, but* DEREK *pulls her frantically back.*)

DEREK. But in whose favor? Who gets the money—the estate—the stocks and bonds—?!

J.D. I'm sorry, Derek, you know I cannot reveal that information. Ethics, my boy, professional ethics.

DEREK. Damn your ethics! Who hits the Stratton jackpot?!

J.D. My lips are sealed.

SYLVIA. Till the will is read?

J.D. Of course.

DEREK. (*Calming himself with an effort.*) Look—let me put it this way—is it George?

J.D. No.

SYLVIA. Derek?

J.D. No.

DEREK. You?

SYLVIA. The servants?

DEREK. The cook?

J.D. (*Shaking head.*) No, no, no.

DEREK. Then who can it possibly . . . ? Oh, no. Not that?! (J.D. *fidgets.*) Look me in the eye, Culver. Is it—Miss Brent?

J.D. (*Beat; then:*) I can't tell you that.

(SYLVIA *and* DEREK *exchange a look of glum comprehension and sag side by side onto the sofa;* HERBERT SANDERS, *a middle-aged butler in full livery, enters from hall.*)

SANDERS. Ms. Culver, ma'am, Mister Stratton requires your presence in his room.

J.D. (*Galvanized, grabs coat, heads for hall.*) Sorry to rush off like this, but business is business! (*Exits,* SANDERS *following her out.*)

DEREK. It seems as if Peggy Brent has struck it rich at the Strattons! Funny, she never impressed me as the gold-digging type—which is probably why she's a success at it. So different from you.

SYLVIA. (*Stands angrily.*) I could have hit the jackpot myself if I hadn't been playing with a *slug!*

DEREK. (*Impatiently pulls her back down beside him.*) All is not yet lost. We still have a few hours before Uncle Oliver heads for the Himalayas!

SYLVIA. Dearest, the new will was drawn up yesterday. As far as your uncle is concerned, the time is past to woo his favor—or cut his throat.

DEREK. But there's all the time in the world for me to woo the new heiress!

SYLVIA. (*Coldly.*) How nice for *you!*

DEREK. Now, Sylvia, don't take that attitude. I shall most certainly provide you a place in my plans.

SYLVIA. I don't doubt it. There you'll be with Peggy, sipping champagne at some posh New York nitery—and I'll be right there at your side—selling cigarettes!

DEREK. Surely, darling, you don't think that my wooing Peggy would make a difference between *us?*

SYLVIA. Do you mean to say that you expect things to keep on, just like always, after you've married Peggy?!

DEREK. (*Jumps to his feet.*) Married Peggy?! Who said anything about *marrying* her?!

SYLVIA. How else do you propose to pry the money out of her hot little hands?

DEREK. I do not propose to pry. When I have done with her, she shall pour the money right into my lap.

SYLVIA. Or onto your head?

DEREK. (*Paces, thinking aloud.*) Don't be idiotic. I intend to appeal to her finer feelings. She has a soft spot in her heart for the down-and-out. A simple hard-luck story should turn the trick—young nephew, losing his rightful inheritance to a stranger—too proud to ask for charity—

SYLVIA. —too lazy to go to work—

DEREK. (*Stops pacing, exasperated.*) You have no confidence in my genius.

SYLVIA. Not if it comes from your *uncle's* side of the family! It seems to me that when a man is as rich as your uncle, with all the comforts that modern civilization and indoor plumbing can provide, and then he chucks it all to become an apprentice lama in a Tibetan monastery, there's a screw loose someplace, and it's not in his Rolls Royce!

DEREK. (*Drops down beside her, takes her hands.*) Darling, have faith in me. I'll get that money for us somehow. Peggy is a kindhearted, gentle creature, devoted to the alleviation of human suffering—and believe me, I'm suffering!

SYLVIA. Now just prove you're human, and it's in the bag! (*Rises to go, but he grabs her hand; she hesitates.*)

DEREK. Now, now, dearest, you're overwrought. Just leave everything to me! (*Behind them, GEORGE enters unobserved from garden.*) Peggy Brent will not inherit the Stratton estate!

GEORGE. Peggy—?! Who said she *would* inherit it?! (*They both react on hearing his voice, DEREK coming to his feet.*)

SYLVIA. *Only* J.D. Culver, your father's *attorney*, but what would *she* know?!

DEREK. (*Follows SYLVIA Upstage Left to GEORGE.*) Now, Sylvia, I told you that *I* wanted to break the bad news to George!

SYLVIA. That figures.

DEREK. I *mean*, Sylvia, that I would have eased the blow. As his cousin and dear friend, I would have first prepared him for the shock, poor lad.

GEORGE. What is all this? What's happened?

SYLVIA. Thanks to the machiavellian machinations of a mincing Mata Hari, your father's fat head has been turned to the tune of forty million bucks!

DEREK. Forty million bucks is not a tune—it's at least seven symphonies!

GEORGE. I still don't understand.

DEREK. Thanks to Peggy the Party Pooper, your pinheaded Poppa has signed a paper that leaves you a pauper!

SYLVIA. Thank you, Edgar A. Guest.

GEORGE. You mean—?

SYLVIA. Oliver—probably in one of his lucid moments—has cut you and Derek out of his will, and left kit and kaboodle to Florence Nightingale, otherwise known as Our Miss Brent!

GEORGE. But—I'm his own son, his flesh-and-blood heir—why would he leave everything to Miss Brent?

(SYLVIA *and* DEREK *converge upon him, each clutching an arm, alternating lines rapidly into his ears, with quick and urgent delivery, while he stares out front in growing alarm.*)

SYLVIA. Who sat up nights with him and held his hand—?

DEREK. Who waked him in the morning with a cheery smile and tucked him in at night—?

SYLVIA. Who waited on him hand and foot—

DEREK. Day and night—

SYLVIA. Rain or shine—?

DEREK. And who, in the still of the evening, twined his graying hair about her slim strong fingers—

SYLVIA. And whispered sweet nothings into his waxy ears—?

GEORGE. Is *that* what she was doing in his room every night?!

SYLVIA. She wasn't reading him *The Three Bears*.

DEREK. Face the facts. Miss Peggy Brent is an attractive woman.

SYLVIA. And Oliver Stratton is a *man*, spelled p-u-t-t-y!

GEORGE. (*His eye grim, his jaw jutted, steps forward from their grasp.*) She shan't get away with it. I shall stop her. I shall worm my way into her heartless heart—make violent love to her to expose her as the dark schemer she is—kiss her until she screams for mercy—!

SYLVIA. (*With a look at* DEREK.) You Strattons are all alike.

OLIVER. (*Off.*) The last I saw of George he was looking for *you*, Miss Brent. Perhaps he's in the library—

SYLVIA. (*Clasps her hands to her chest.*) Hark, it's the voice of the Gestapo! I really must fly! (*Bolts for garden doors*, DEREK *following.*)

DEREK. Shall I drive you to the station?

SYLVIA. No need, the bus stops just beyond your garden gate. You stay here and protect our interests!

DEREK. (*Exiting to garden with her.*) At least let me escort you down the primrose path.

SYLVIA. (*As they move Left, out of sight.*) Here we go again!

PEGGY. (*As she—a pretty young thing in nurse's uniform—and* OLIVER—*a pretty-old thing in a somber suit—enter from hall.*) Oh, there you are, George. Your father and I were just looking for you. There isn't much more time to say goodbye.

OLIVER. Nonsense. George is young. He'll forget. He's got a good job, good future, and the name of Stratton. He'll get by. And someday, he will meet a woman—and then at last he'll understand why I'm doing—what I'm doing . . . ! (SANDERS *enters from hall.*)

SANDERS. Mister Stratton, sir—a person is here.

OLIVER. What do you mean, a person?

SANDERS. I believe the gentleman's name is Wu Chang, sir.

OLIVER. Wu Chang! I wasn't expecting him for hours! Tell him I'll be right there! (*As* SANDERS *exits to hall:*) Can you imagine! All the way from Tibet, just to pick me up! . . . Oh, George, would you tell cook there'll be another guest at dinner—?

GEORGE. (*Darkly.*) Cook is making individual desserts.

OLIVER. Oh. Um. Well—tell her anyhow, then duck! (*As* GEORGE *exits to hall:*) My dear, will you excuse me while I greet my guest?

PEGGY. Of course. I'm really looking forward to meeting this man.

OLIVER. Oh, you shall, you shall—as soon as the family is assembled in here.

PEGGY. (*Turns slightly away, thoughtful; then:*) This woman you loved—was she pretty?

OLIVER. (*Never thought about it before, so muses aloud:*) She had—uh—an inner beauty. On the surface I suppose you'd say she was not quite so—oh—as attractive as—well—she was rather drab, now that I think of it—but something shone through her plain features that made her light up—not light enough to see her too well, unhappily. I never did get a really good look at her face. It was very dark on deck.

PEGGY. Did you ever think—that your behavior is rather foolish—?

OLIVER. You mean my going off this way? I daresay you're right—but that's what love does to people. My money, my home, my family—none of them matter if I cannot have *her*. That's why I'm going to Tibet—to try to forget.

PEGGY. But isn't there some way—

OLIVER. I've exhausted them all. It's as though she vanished from the face of the earth.

PEGGY. (*Shyly faces him.*) You know, Oliver, I feel rather guilty—about my job here. You weren't really sick—

OLIVER. Not physically, no. But a broken heart doesn't show up on the x-rays. You were invaluable. You gave me the will to go on.

PEGGY. Nonsense. If I somehow kept you in good spirits—

OLIVER. Don't underrate yourself, my dear. Don't ever do that. You know—if I'd been a younger man when you came along . . . ! But I'm keeping Wu Chang waiting! I'll be back presently. (*Exits to hall.*)

PEGGY. The poor man. The poor silly man. (*Sits on sofa;* DEREK *enters from garden, sees her, moves to a vantage point just above table, looking at her.*)

DEREK. You seem tired, Peggy.

PEGGY. (*With a half-turn to see who is speaking.*) Oh, Derek. Yes, you're right. Tired—and a bit sad. Your uncle—

DEREK. Yes, it's a pity, but once Oliver makes up his mind— (*Stops as she abruptly buries her face in her hands.*) Why—what's the matter?

PEGGY. I—I suppose it's the suddenness of the thing— and the silliness. A man like Oliver, throwing away so much—but there's just no dissuading him—and—I've grown rather fond of him.

DEREK. Say, this is serious! Perhaps—you should lie down or something—?

PEGGY. That's not a bad idea. The strain is making me weary . . .

(PEGGY *reclines on sofa, a forearm across her eyes;* JANE *enters from hall, Upstage of* DEREK, *who does not notice her, with a featherduster; she cannot see* PEGGY *on sofa, and moves to dust painting and books, but stops as* DEREK *speaks; we can see at once that she believes him to be speaking to her.*)

DEREK. My dear—I have something to say to you—no, don't say a word, or I won't be able to finish. Since you first came to work for us, I haven't been blind to your charm. I suppose you'll say that it's all part of your job, but you'll be wrong. You have a charm that exceeds the requirements of your position. When you come into a room, it lights up, somehow, and I feel that— No, please don't speak, not till I've said it all. I know I can't hope that you've noticed the way I feel, but someday, in the near future, I hope you might find it in your heart to care just a little for me, as I do for you . . . ?

JANE. (*Unable to contain herself.*) Oh, Master Derek! I never *dreamed*—! (*Flings herself, featherduster and all, about his neck.*)

DEREK. (*Struggling, in shock.*) Jane! What are you doing! Have you taken leave of your senses? Confound it, unhand me!

PEGGY. (*Sits up.*) What—? Oh, Jane! I thought we were alone.

DEREK. (*Finally prying* JANE *loose.*) So did I!

JANE. (*Now icily reserved.*) I beg your pardon, sir.

DEREK. No, Jane, I beg yours. That was extremely stupid of me.

JANE. I quite agree, sir! (*Exits haughtily to hall.*)

DEREK. I feel like such a fool—!

PEGGY. (*Starts to giggle.*) And you looked so silly, wrestling her off your neck! (*Mimics him.*) "Confound it, unhand me!" (*Goes into nearly hysterical laughter.*)

DEREK. I suppose the whole thing did look a bit ridiculous— (*Abruptly joins in her laughter.*) How will I ever face Jane again! Playing pingpong with her heart!

PEGGY. (*Recovering from laughter.*) Well, it must be nice to know the servants think well of you. (*He laughs again, starts down around sofa to her.*) And Derek—what you said to me—I'll—think it over.

DEREK. (*Sits beside her, turned to face her.*) Then—I have a chance—?

PEGGY. (*Gently takes his hands.*) It's been a bit too abrupt for me to say, Derek. But there certainly is a possibility. I'm flattered that you've noticed me. (SYLVIA *enters from garden, gets her forgotten purse from desk, then stops in reaction to tableau.*) I always thought that you and Sylvia—

DEREK. Sylvia? Ha! It is she who desires *me*, Peggy, not I *her*. Oh, she's amusing enough, I suppose—but then, so is a flea circus! (*If* SYLVIA'S *looks could kill,* DEREK *would now be a violently mangled corpse; he suddenly pulls* PEGGY *to him, ardently.*) Oh, Peggy, it is you I want! Only you! No one but you! (*Kisses her.*)

PEGGY. (*Pulls back.*) Derek! Kissing is terribly unsanitary!

DEREK. I have a family-size bottle of Listerine in my room. We can go up there afterwards, and gargle hand-in-hand! (*Kisses her again.*)

PEGGY. (*Pulls free again, and says sardonically:*) And if you take me out, should I pack a roll of Sucrets? (*But DEREK has just caught sight of SYLVIA, who turns in fury and exits to garden; he jumps up and starts after her.*)

DEREK. Uh, yes, certainly, anything you say. Excuse me! (*Exits after SYLVIA, fast; as PEGGY looks after him in some bewilderment, GEORGE enters from hall.*)

GEORGE. Hello, Peggy—have you seen Derek—?

PEGGY. I think he just went to his room to gargle.

GEORGE. (*His manner changing slightly.*) Then we are—alone? You and I—?

PEGGY. (*Apprehensive, not sure why.*) Yes—yes, I suppose we are, George . . . ?

GEORGE. Good. Because— (*Moves down to right end of sofa, smiling down upon her.*) My dear, I have something to say to you—no, don't say a word, or I won't be able to finish. Since you first came to work for us, I haven't been blind to your charm—

PEGGY. (*Naturally both fascinated and suspicious.*) Is that a fact!

GEORGE. I suppose you'll say that it's all part of your job, but you'll be wrong. You have a charm that—

PEGGY. (*Will rise on her line.*) I have a charm that exceeds the requirements of my position—?

GEORGE. Uh. *Yes* . . . But—?!

PEGGY. And when I come into a room, it lights up, somehow, and—?

GEORGE. Yes, that's right, but—how in the world did you know what I—?

PEGGY. I have such an eerie feeling—as if history were repeating itself . . .

GEORGE. I beg your pardon—?

PEGGY. George, what is going on here? Is that an original speech?

GEORGE. (*Quite flustered and abashed, now.*) Well—as a matter of fact—no.

PEGGY. Ah! Then where—?

GEORGE. Derek and I were in a play in college, once, where the leading man was in love with the governess, and—

PEGGY. (*Laughs with delight.*) *Now* it comes out! Look— if I might mimic Priscilla Mullen—speak for yourself, George!

GEORGE. (*Grins wryly, scratches briefly behind one ear.*) I guess it *was* a bit theatrical, wasn't it!

PEGGY. (*Takes his hands, makes him sit down beside her on sofa.*) Come on, boy—sit thee down here beside me and spill what's buzzing in your brain—but in your own words, for heaven's sake!

GEORGE. (*Takes a breath for courage, considers, then says:*) All right. You're pretty. You're charming. You're fun to be with. I like you. When you're not around, I wish you were. There. Isn't that the flattest speech you ever heard?

PEGGY. (*Sincerely.*) Cyrano de Bergerac couldn't top it. (*Facetiously.*) And may I go off the deep end and say that I have not exactly been blind to *your* charms, either? When you come into a room, it lights up, somehow, and—

GEORGE. Please! Stop. I surrender, Peggy.

PEGGY. I like you to call me Peggy. I feel like part of the family. When you call me Miss Brent, I feel like part of the furniture.

GEORGE. Do I sound bad as all that?

PEGGY. Habitually! But the way you are now—without that icy armor plate you normally wear—you're, well, kind of nice, George . . . dear George . . . dear sweet George . . . (*They melt into a terrific clinch and kiss, just as* JANE *enters from hall; she sees them, reacts, clears her throat.*)

JANE. Master Derek—

GEORGE. (*Coming out of clinch and shifting to face her.*) It is I, Jane. Derek has gone a-gargling.

JANE. (*A bit startled by his identity.*) Oh. Well. Uh— dinner is served. (*Almost turns, but hesitates.*)

GEORGE. Is there anything the matter, Jane—?

JANE. (*Not certain how to explain her confusion.*) No, sir—not really—only— Well, a person certainly needs a program to know who's up at bat around here! (*Exits huffily to hall.*)

GEORGE. Now, what could she mean by that?

PEGGY. (*Who knows, and who'd rather not explain.*) Say, shall we go in to dinner? Cook doesn't like to be kept waiting! (*Takes his arm, pulls him hallward.*)

GEORGE. But what did Jane mean about being up at bat?

PEGGY. (*As she tows him out into hall.*) Who knows? Maybe she noticed you were getting to first base! (*They are barely gone when an angry* SYLVIA, *followed by a desperately unhappy* DEREK, *come swiftly in from garden.*)

SYLVIA. (*In mid-speech as they enter.*) —and as far as I'm concerned, you can lose every red cent of that inheritance. If you love me, then announce our engagement to everyone, Oliver included. I'm sick of sneaking through the shrubbery, throwing pebbles at your window, disguising my voice when I telephone—!

DEREK. (*Pulls her anxiously to a stop, just above table.*) Wait! Darling, you know I can't do that. It would spoil everything. I have Peggy right where I want her, now, and—

SYLVIA. (*Turns to face him, furious.*) The only way you'll get any money from that woman is to beat her over the head with a chair-leg and take it! Will you please *forget* all this sordid scheming and announce our engagement, or not?! Because, believe me, Derek Stratton, if you don't, then there *is* no engagement!

DEREK. Darling, darling, you just don't understand!

SYLVIA. What's to understand?! There's me, and there's

Miss Brent, you've made your choice, and that's that! The least you could do is spare me the biological details!

DEREK. No-no-no, listen, you've got it all wrong. (*More calmly.*) Sylvia—why do you suppose Uncle Oliver disapproves of you so heartily?

SYLVIA. I've never stuck around long enough to ask him. I suppose because I'm not on your social level.

DEREK. Not at all. Oliver is really very tolerant about people's status in society.

SYLVIA. Then why? Why does he go purple when he catches a glimpse of me? What have I got, the plague?

DEREK. Something much worse, in Oliver's eyes: You have *me!*

SYLVIA. You? But—Derek—?

DEREK. (*Patiently.*) It's quite simple. Uncle Oliver reasons that since I am a wastrel, a no-good, and general all-around bum, no *worthwhile* woman would look twice at me. Since you obviously adore me, he's certain *you* are up to no good, do you see? He probably assumes you are after my money.

SYLVIA. But, Derek—you *have* no money!

DEREK. I'll *get* some, if you don't louse things up! Don't you see—if Oliver once suspects that *Peggy* is nuts about me—

SYLVIA. He'll disapprove of *her!* And change his will *back!* Is that it?

DEREK. Exactly! *Now* do you see why I can't announce our engagement?!

SYLVIA. I—I'm beginning to—but—this isn't a trick? I mean, you won't go ahead and marry her or anything?

DEREK. Sylvia, you have my word as a gentleman, I love only you! On my honor!

SYLVIA. You haven't been a gentleman since the day I *met* you! And as for your honor—! (*Before he can reply,* OLIVER *enters from hall; both freeze.*)

OLIVER. Ah, there you are, Derek! Have you seen Peggy

and—and— Miss Crane! Derek, I distinctly told you that woman was never to set foot in my house again!

DEREK. But—Uncle—your last night at home—!

OLIVER. I'd like it to be a pleasant one, if you don't mind! Young lady, you will do me the courtesy of—

SYLVIA. (*Turning on the kilowatts.*) Leaving? Ah, but Mister Stratton, how can I? I realize that you think little of me, and I daresay you have grounds, but, from all that Derek has told me of you, I can't help but admire you tremendously!

OLIVER. Honeyed words have no power to—to— Admire?

DEREK. Tremendously.

SYLVIA. And so, now, although I have not the right, since you have forbidden me to come here, I just had to see you, just this once more. You are leaving tonight, and—well—I thought that, no matter what you did to me, I'd have to look upon your noble face for one last time, to gather a memory I could hold and cherish forever!

OLIVER. Dear lady . . . I didn't realize . . . I had no idea . . .

SYLVIA. (*Wiping away an imaginary tear, holds up a hand.*) No. You're quite right. I should not have come. I only felt that I could not let you depart without my risking your displeasure to come here and tell you what has been burning in my heart these many months. (*Solemnly tragic.*) And now it is said. And now I shall go. (*Turns toward garden doors.*)

OLIVER. Oh, come now, it's not so bad as all that—! (*She waits, her back to him, a triumphant smile on her lips.*) I mean—I'm sure that, on my last night here, I should be a bit more—um—*tolerant* of people. Besides, right now, it is as though I'd seen you for the first time, somehow, and I find that you are quite—um—

DEREK. (*Helpfully.*) —tolerable?

SYLVIA. (*Lays her hand upon* DEREK'S *arm.*) Derek—I

have disturbed this marvelous man quite enough. Will you please see me home?

DEREK. (*Incredulous.*) To the Bronx?!

OLIVER. Wait! Derek, I have been a hard-hearted old fool. By all means, Miss Crane, stay. Stay for dinner! Derek, go tell cook there will be one more guest for dinner—

DEREK. Cook is making individual desserts . . .

OLIVER. Oh, drat, I forgot. Well—pop your head in the kitchen, shout it fast, then run!

DEREK. (*Darkly.*) Cook won't like it. (*Exits to hall; SYLVIA slowly turns to face OLIVER.*)

SYLVIA. You know—underneath that gruff exterior, you're rather nice.

OLIVER. Oh—shucks, Miss Crane!

SYLVIA. "Sylvia." Please.

OLIVER. It's a lovely name. For a lovely woman. You know, if I were a younger man—oh well, no point in mulling it over. I leave for Tibet, tonight, and that's that.

SYLVIA. Oliver—how—how *can* you leave all this, to— to become a monk?

OLIVER. Ah, if you had the secret sorrow I have, you'd become a monk, too.

SYLVIA. (*Leaves purse on table, leads him to sit on sofa.*) Tell me about it. It's a woman, isn't it! It would have to be a woman!

OLIVER. Yes. Yes, you're right. It is a woman. A one-of-a-kind woman. Drab, but charming. Middle-aged, but kind. Not too bright, but gentle.

SYLVIA. (*Nods understandingly.*) You loved her and she didn't love back.

OLIVER. (*Shakes head.*) Oh, yes, she did. She said so. But then—!

SYLVIA. Something happened . . . ?

OLIVER. (*Sighs.*) Yes. Something that— Shall I tell you about it?

SYLVIA. (*Gently pillowing his head upon her shoulder.*) If it will help the hurt. Tell me, Oliver. Tell me all.

OLIVER. (*Wistfully reminiscing.*) I was returning from Europe. The ship was cruising gently through the night. There was a moon, and a breeze blowing softly through the blue-velvet air. I was standing on the foredeck, looking at the sea, and thinking about life—and love—and the meaning of it all. I turned my head . . .

SYLVIA. And there she was.

OLIVER. Yes.

SYLVIA. Staring at the stars—?

OLIVER. Well, actually, she was being sick over the rail. Ah, but when she finally straightened up, our eyes met. Then suddenly, her hand closed over my own, on the rail. Something inside of me surged and roared, and I could tell she felt the same way. And the next moment—

SYLVIA. Yes . . . ?

OLIVER. We were *both* being sick over the rail. After that, of course, ours was a whirlwind romance. We had both lost our hearts!

SYLVIA. Among other things.

OLIVER. Exactly. We exchanged remedies for hours on end. I knew I couldn't let it all end there. I had to see her again. The ship was to dock the next morning. I took down her name and address on the inside of a gum wrapper— Juicy Fruit—and put it into my pocket.

SYLVIA. And then—?

OLIVER. Morning came. The ship docked. We disembarked. Crowds, the fuss with customs, the hurry and all . . . I didn't catch sight of her. And then, when I returned home here, and took the gum wrapper from my pocket—!

SYLVIA. Yes, Oliver, yes—?

OLIVER. The ink had smeared. I couldn't read it. I had been smuggling in a small bottle of French perfume. It had popped its cork, and run all over the gum wrapper, leaving the sweet smell of total illegibility!

SYLVIA. (*Nods solemnly.*) Crime does not pay.

OLIVER. Well put, well put. I called in detectives, put ads in all the papers, had leaflets scattered from planes, bought advertising space upon billboards, in theatre programs, inside fortune cookies—but to no avail.

SYLVIA. She didn't respond?

OLIVER. Actually, how could she? I didn't recall her name, so I couldn't very well put that in the messages. It was night on the boat deck, and I wasn't feeling too steady, so I didn't see her well enough to furnish the detectives with a description. All I could recall was her voice, her beautiful voice, but when I tried imitating it for the detectives, they merely laughed. Oh, many a woman replied to my message, but never the right one. And so—

SYLVIA. You abandoned all hope.

OLIVER. Yes. What was left for me? Except—to try to forget. And so—that is why I am going to become a monk. I'll shave my head and eyebrows, get a robe and ricebowl, sit on a rock—and sigh a lot.

SYLVIA. Ah, but must you? Go so far for your forgetfulness, I mean? With the right person—the right *woman*—to help you, you could—you could forget right here! Right here on Long Island—in this house—in this room—on this sofa—!

OLIVER. (*Lifts his head from her shoulder, stares at her.*) Sylvia! You mean yourself, don't you! You would sacrifice your sweet youth to comfort an old man like me.

SYLVIA. Yes. Yes, I would!

OLIVER. I couldn't let you do that!

SYLVIA. Yes. Yes, you could!

OLIVER. I shouldn't even consider it!

SYLVIA. Yes. Yes, you should!

OLIVER. It's—it's too noble of you . . .

SYLVIA. Let me *try*, at least! (*Starts to twine his hair about her fingers, playfully.*) Little by little, day by day, I can force myself to give you the necessary distractions, and—

OLIVER. Uh . . . well . . . I suppose . . . perhaps . . . No! It's too late. Wu Chang is here. I can't send him back emptyhanded. He's come halfway around the world to get me. Last week, you might have convinced me. But now—I am irrevocably committed.

SYLVIA. Nothing is irrevocable! If you explain to this Wu Chang—

OLIVER. You don't understand—he is a recruiter. I read his ad in the New York Times. He gets points for everyone he brings in, toward his retirement. He says getting me will put him over the top. So, really—

SYLVIA. Please, Oliver—at least let me *try* to win your heart! I'm sure that—

OLIVER. (*Pats her shoulder, paternally.*) Yes, yes you could win my heart—if I had not already lost it—to her! (SANDERS *enters from hall, his manner nervous.*)

SYLVIA. But Oliver—

SANDERS. Excuse me, Mister Stratton, sir—second call for dinner!

OLIVER. (*Jumps up.*) Second?! Good heavens, cook will be furious! Thank you, Sanders! (*Extends his arm as* SYLVIA *stands.*) My dear—?

SYLVIA. (*Taking his arm.*) Thank you, Oliver. (*Looks up as* PEGGY *and* GEORGE *enter from hall.*)

PEGGY. Oliver, I have devastating news!

OLIVER. Why, Peggy, what is it?

PEGGY. Cook prepared the roast with garlic!

OLIVER. But, Peggy, I like garlic.

PEGGY. But garlic doesn't like you. I'm still your nurse, and I forbid you to eat a bite of it. Why, if you took a boat trip with that in your stomach, you'd never reach Tibet alive!

GEORGE. She's right, Oliver. I remember that time we brought home the pepperoni pizza, and you were up half the night, retching and heaving—

SYLVIA. George! Please!

OLIVER. My dears, nothing could upset me tonight. This

lama, Wu Chang, is a man of contemplation, peace and harmony. I guarantee you, just to have him walk into a room brings the most incredible serenity! When I am under his influence, not even garlic can upset me.

PEGGY. Oliver, contemplating your navel won't alleviate acute gastritis!

SYLVIA. Will you all please shut up while I still have an appetite left?!

OLIVER. Listen, all of you, mere words tell you nothing. I shall go and bring Wu Chang here. I promise you that when he enters through that door, this will be a place of peace and harmony and serenity, as his spell enfolds you like a bright, golden cloud! I'll be right back! (*Nearly bumps into* DEREK, *just entering from hall.*) Oops, sorry.

DEREK. (*Watching him exit.*) Where's he off to? I hope nobody *else* is staying for dinner. Cook was most upset when I told her about Sylvia.

PEGGY. Sylvia? Staying for dinner? Do you mean—she and Oliver are on friendly terms at last?

SYLVIA. *Very.* Kind of rocks *your* applecart, doesn't it!

PEGGY. George, what is she talking about?

GEORGE. (*Miserable.*) Oh—Peggy—stop it, please. I wish things could be different, but—well, I know what you've done. But I want you to know—I forgive you.

PEGGY. Thanks a heap. What are you forgiving me *for?* Or am I supposed to know?

SYLVIA. I suppose it's slipped your mind that you've had your eye on the Stratton fortune ever since you arrived here?

PEGGY. *What?!*

SYLVIA. I suppose you and old Oliver haven't been playing footsie upstairs when you were supposedly taking his temperature?

PEGGY. That's so ridiculous I won't even deny it!

DEREK. See, George? She won't deny it!

PEGGY. Listen, Derek, your uncle is my employer, and that's *all* he is!

GEORGE. You didn't tell him you were fond of him?

PEGGY. Suppose I *did?!* I *am* fond of him! Aren't *you?*

DEREK. George's devotion to Oliver is notoriously unselfish!

PEGGY. And mine isn't?!

SYLVIA. See, George, she admits it! (JANE *gallops in from hall, snaps to attention near door.*)

JANE. Last call for dinner! Cook is blowing her top!

PEGGY. (*To* DEREK *and* SYLVIA.) You're not only hateful, you're stupid!

JANE. I don't have to stand for that kind of talk! (J.D. *enters from hall.*)

J.D. Is Wu Chang in here?

GEORGE. Peggy, I hate to do this, but— J.D., isn't it true that Peggy is my father's sole heir?

JANE. (*Still nursing her erroneous sorrow.*) I work hard, and I don't deserve to be shouted at! Especially by—

PEGGY. (*Responding to* GEORGE.) *Me?*

JANE. (*On same wrong track.*) Who else?!

J.D. Well, Peggy, it was supposed to be a secret, but—

JANE. I slave, I toil, I labor—

GEORGE. There, Peggy, you *see?*

PEGGY. But I didn't *know!*

JANE. That's because you never *watch* me!

PEGGY. (*Half-catching this.*) What—?

GEORGE. Didn't know?!

J.D. How could she know? Until tonight, the only ones who knew were myself and Oliver!

JANE. All I ever asked was a little consideration—

GEORGE. Until *tonight?!*

JANE. *Even* tonight!

GEORGE. (*Half-catching this.*) What—?

PEGGY. Ms. Culver, who found *out* tonight—?

J.D. Derek tricked it out of me.

GEORGE. Derek! Aha!

JANE. He's been up to all *sorts* of tricks, tonight!

DEREK. Now, George, take it easy—

GEORGE. You called this sweet innocent woman a gold-digger!

JANE. That's not *all* he called me!

GEORGE. What—?

DEREK. (*Apprehensive, since* GEORGE *looks ready for a brawl.*) Now, George—if I happened, by merest chance, to give you the impression—

GEORGE. (*Lunges at* DEREK.) Why, you louse!

SYLVIA. (*Trying to come between them.*) Please—!

DEREK. (*Swings at* GEORGE, *on:*) Who's a louse?! (*His fist neatly connects with* SYLVIA'S *eye, and she topples flat on her back onto the sofa, out cold;* PEGGY, *the nurse in her uppermost, sits on edge of sofa to take her pulse.*)

JANE. Listen, everyone—cook is just about at the boiling point—!

GEORGE. Hit a defenseless woman, will you?!

DEREK. (*Sparring with him.*) I already *did!*

(DEREK *grabs up ice bucket to crown* GEORGE; JANE *screams and faints back into* J.D.'s *arms; distracted,* DEREK *is set upon by* GEORGE, *who gets him to floor and begins choking him.*)

PEGGY. (*Left hand on* SYLVIA'S *wrist, looks blankly at her own right wrist, which is bare, then asks brightly.*) Has anybody got a watch?

J.D. (*Valiantly trying to support the comatose* JANE.) What does it matter what *time* it is?

GEORGE. (*Not only choking* DEREK, *but pounding his head on the carpet.*) Derek's time is running out, anyway!

PEGGY. (*Anxiously chafing* SYLVIA'S *wrist between her palms.*) Won't somebody *help* me—?

J.D. Somebody help *me!*

DEREK. (*Through a constricted throat.*) How about helping *me?!*

(*And as all three start to ad-lib "Help!" over and over,*
OLIVER *enters from hall with* WU CHANG, *a short man
whose face is almost hidden in his hooded robe;* ALL
freeze in place, and go silent, for:)

OLIVER. (*Speaking as he enters:*) Can't you feel the serenity already—?! (*Then he reacts to the tableau, and as*
GEORGE, PEGGY *and* J.D. *stare at him in confusion*—)

Blackout

ACT ONE

SCENE 2

The dining room of the Stratton mansion.* [*This is a half-
stage setting, accomplished by cast and crew working
like lightning to 1) move desk and chair Upstage near
garden doors, 2) set flowers, liquor, etc. from tabletop
onto seat of sofa, then flip over tabletop—which is
actually a hinged board, its underside equipped with
fastened-on tableware, place settings, tablecloth (long
enough to cover front of sofa to floor once in place),
and even a centerpiece if you want one—and have
everybody bring the other Onstage chairs to 3) rest
around "dining table" with one chair at each end, and
five chairs along Upstage edge, and then 4) seven filled
stemmed goblets of wine are set in place for diners,
and 5) a curtain—or even a long folding screen—
comes into place just Upstage of the five chairs, for
dining-room wall. At extreme Left, this divider reaches
almost to Left wall, but at Right, enough space is left to
expose hall door, which is now the "kitchen door."*]

---

* See "RECOMMENDATIONS" at end of play.

JANE *is standing looking out into kitchen, in mid-conversation with the cook, holding a water pitcher.*

JANE. Yes, Mildred, they're finally coming—unless another fistfight's started. You sure you got seven desserts? I can't think of anybody else who might drop in, but maybe you should've made an extra one, just in case— . . . Mildred, don't stand there with your face getting that color, I was only kidding! (*Glances toward Left, moves swiftly to set pitcher on table.*) Whoops, here they come. I'd better start serving!

(*She exits to kitchen, fast;* DEREK *and* SYLVIA *enter from Left—the "hall"—dressed as before, but* SYLVIA *wears a pair of very large and dark sunglasses.* [*NOTE: Seating arrangement, when all are in place, will be, from Right:* OLIVER, J.D., PEGGY, DEREK, SYLVIA, GEORGE *and* WU.])

DEREK. (*Genuinely solicitous.*) Does it hurt much, darling?

SYLVIA. (*Sarcastically.*) No, of course not! I *like* a punch in the eye now and then—it keeps me on my toes!

DEREK. Please don't take that attitude!

SYLVIA. What attitude is one *supposed* to take when the man one loves hauls off and *belts* one one?

DEREK. That blow was intended for George.

SYLVIA. I wish he'd succeeded in strangling you!

DEREK. You don't mean that.

SYLVIA. No, you're right. Strangling is too good for you. I wish he'd set fire to your necktie!

DEREK. You'd stand by and watch a thing like that?

SYLVIA. Hell, no! I'd grab a newspaper and fan the flames!

DEREK. You're joking.

SYLVIA. Sure I'm joking. Nero was joking. Mrs.
O'Leary's cow was joking.

DEREK. Sylvia—are you upset with me?

SYLVIA. (*Laughs hollowly.*) Upset? Why should I be
upset? All you've done tonight is made love to another
woman, compared me to a flea circus, and knocked me cold
with a left jab!

DEREK. That was a right hook. And I'm sorry. Maybe I
could go and ask cook for a piece of beefsteak for that eye.

SYLVIA. And maybe you'd come back with your individual dessert on your head.

DEREK. (*With an uneasy glance kitchenward.*) She *is* a
bit touchy, tonight . . . Here, let me see that eye— (*Lifts
glasses to expose a masterpiece of a shiner.*)

SYLVIA. Isn't it lovely? My left eye, that I've had ever
since I was a little girl, gleaming like a pool of deep blue
water—cunningly set in the center of a burnt doughnut!
(*Tilts glasses back in place to hide the sight.*)

DEREK. Darling, if there's anything I can do—?

SYLVIA. There is. Set fire to your necktie and hand me a
newspaper!

DEREK. Sylvia, don't be childish!

SYLVIA. *I'm* being childish?! I suppose telling George
Peggy is a gold-digger is adult behavior? I suppose calling
me a flea circus is the mark of a mature man? I suppose
bashing in the eye of the woman you profess to love is the
pinnacle of emotional stability?

DEREK. Sylvia, you are being idiotic, unreasonable and
illogical!

SYLVIA. Of course I am! I'm a woman!

DEREK. (*Takes her shoulders.*) You know something—
you're right! (*Kisses her gently but firmly; then, when he
stops:*)

SYLVIA. Why did you do that—?

DEREK. Why did you do that back—?

SYLVIA. (*Turns away, nearly in tears.*) It must be love. I know it sounds silly, considering my chances, but it's the only explanation—my soul is bared, cards are on the table, and the cat is out of the bag. I adore you, you louse! (*Starts to sniffle; he turns her tenderly to face him.*)

DEREK. This is all Peggy's fault!

SYLVIA. Stop passing the buck! Peggy didn't know a thing about the will!

DEREK. But if she had, I would have been right, and George wouldn't have tried to belt me, and you wouldn't have gotten popped in the eye.

SYLVIA. *Now* who's being illogical?!

DEREK. Listen, the others will be here soon—close your pretty little painted mouth and I will tell you my new plan.

SYLVIA. Oh, no you don't! Tell me over the phone. I'm getting out of here while I still have *one* good eye!

DEREK. Darling, this can't miss!

SYLVIA. (*A protective palm over her left eye-area.*) The other one didn't!

DEREK. (*Restrains her from leaving.*) It can't fail. Look, Uncle Oliver hates booze-hounds. If Peggy should over-indulge at dinner, he might see her in a new light.

SYLVIA. Her *own?*

DEREK. Don't be sarcastic.

SYLVIA. That was the voice of sanity. Derek, how could we get her to do it? Do I sit on her chest while you ply the flask and funnel?

DEREK. Of course not! We use finesse!

SYLVIA. All right, *you* sit on her chest, while *I*—

DEREK. Sylvia, they're coming! Just follow my lead and help out, okay?

SYLVIA. My heart tells me yes, my good eye tells me no . . . Oh well. Sail on! (OLIVER *enters from* "*hall.*")

OLIVER. Derek, maybe I can get some sense out of *you*—what was that fiasco in the library all about?

DEREK. When George slugged Sylvia, I guess I lost control. (SYLVIA *gapes in surprise.*)

OLIVER. Why would *George* slug Sylvia? . . . I mean, why would *anyone?*

DEREK. Because she implied that Miss Brent put less alcohol on her patients' backs than she did on her own tonsils!

OLIVER. Sylvia—you told George that Miss Brent drinks to excess?

SYLVIA. Not in so many words—I merely said she was the only nurse I knew who could sterilize a wound by breathing on it!

OLIVER. But—I was planning on leaving her my entire estate! . . . Oh, drat, that was supposed to be a surprise!

DEREK. (*Nudges* SYLVIA, *and they both over-register surprise, on:*) Oh, it *was!*

SYLVIA. Yes, indeedy! Gosh!

DEREK. If only Miss Brent were—worthy!

SYLVIA. (*Solicitously patting* OLIVER's *shoulder.*) Don't listen to Derek, Oliver. If you want the Stratton fortune to filter by driblets into the nearest distillery, you just go right ahead and leave everything to Peggy.

OLIVER. Sylvia—Derek—is this some sort of joke—?!

SYLVIA. If it is, why did George slug me?

DEREK. George could never take a joke.

OLIVER. Nonsense. George is a good sport.

SYLVIA. But his favorite sport is boxing.

OLIVER. It's hard to believe. Peggy seems so healthy . . .

SYLVIA. She *is* healthy—alcohol kills germs.

DEREK. One nice thing about being a drunkard—you never get a sore throat.

OLIVER. I still cannot believe—if there were some way to be sure—

DEREK. Oh, but there is. Put her to—the Test! (*Just as*

earlier with GEORGE, SYLVIA *and* DEREK *each clutch him by an arm, leaning in to whisper in fast alternation in his ears.*) Just watch her during dinner . . . every move—

SYLVIA. Every sip—

DEREK. Every gush from the bottle—

SYLVIA. Every tilt of the glass—

DEREK. Every swallow—

SYLVIA. Every belch—

OLIVER. I'll do it! And if what you suggest is true—

DEREK. Yes?

SYLVIA. Yes?

OLIVER. I'll cut her off without a cent!

SYLVIA. And who *will* get the money?

OLIVER. Oh . . . George and Derek, I suppose . . . why do you ask?

SYLVIA. (*Pseudo-casually.*) Just curious.

DEREK. Ah, here comes Miss Brent now! . . . Young, vivacious—

SYLVIA. —and ninety proof.

(GEORGE *and* PEGGY *enter from* "hall"; *she has changed from her uniform to a becoming evening dress; as they enter, she stumbles slightly, and* GEORGE *catches her by the arm.*)

PEGGY. (*With a little laugh.*) Darn these high heels!

DEREK. Of *course* it's the heels.

SYLVIA. *We'll* never tell.

GEORGE. Huh—?

OLIVER. (*To* DEREK *and* SYLVIA.) It may have been an accident. I shall watch and wait.

GEORGE. Wait for what?

OLIVER. (*Coldly.*) A man who would strike a defenseless woman deserves no explanations!

(*As* GEORGE *and* PEGGY *react blankly,* J.D. *and* WU *enter*

*from "hall"; * Wu *hesitates near left end of table, but*
J.D. *will cross below table [others are above it] and*
take her place.)

PEGGY. What's that got to do with George?

OLIVER. And I've got my eye on *you,* too! (*As they react*
again, he sees J.D. *sit down.*) J.D., please! Our guest!
(J.D., *flustered, stands;* OLIVER *gestures* WU *to proper*
chair.) Wu Chang, you shall sit opposite me, at that end.

(*As* WU *does so, everyone else moves to proper place, and*
when he is seated, all will sit; as soon as they are
seated, SYLVIA *picks up her wine glass and stands; all*
the men but WU *immediately stand, too.*)

SYLVIA. Take it easy, boys, I'm not leaving. (*They sit*
again.) I just want to propose a toast.
    OLIVER. I thought women did that sitting down.
    DEREK. No, Uncle, *ladies* do that sitting down.
    SYLVIA. Very funny. Okay, so I'll *sit* and propose a
toast! (*Sits, raises glass, frowns.*) It doesn't feel right.
    OLIVER. Well, you can stand if you prefer.
    DEREK. On your head, if you like.
    SYLVIA. (*Stands serenely.*) If everyone will kindly shut
up a moment)—? (*Sees they are quiet, raises glass.*) To
Oliver Stratton—great man, fond father, loving uncle, good
friend, and future lama. May his spirits always be as high as
the mountains to which he travels tonight! . . . That's it,
folks, drink up!
    GEORGE. (*After they all drink and* SYLVIA *sits, rises.*)
And I have a toast—to my father, a great man, a good
friend, and a good egg in general! (ALL *drink, and as*
GEORGE *sits,* DEREK *stands.*)
    DEREK. And here's another one—to Uncle Oliver, whose
loving kindness to me I shall always remember on those

cold winter nights when I'm out on some windswept street
corner selling pencils!

(ALL *laugh, and—unseen except by* J.D., DEREK *dumps
        remainder of his own wine into* PEGGY'S *glass, then
        fakes draining his glass as all drink except* J.D., *who
        watches* DEREK *sit; then:*)

J.D. Derek, why did you do that?

DEREK. (*Trapped, blurts:*) Uh—old Spanish custom!

J.D. You're not Spanish.

SYLVIA. The wine is! It's manzanilla!

GEORGE. I thought manzanilla was an olive?

PEGGY. Isn't that the black kind?

DEREK. I'm sure they come in green, too.

OLIVER. Seems to me they come in all colors.

SYLVIA. Well, live and learn.

J.D. Derek—?

DEREK. . . . Yes, J.D.?

J.D. What was I just going to ask you?

SYLVIA. How would Derek know?

J.D. Well, that's true enough . . . maybe it will come
back to me. (JANE *enters from kitchen.*)

JANE. Shall I serve the soup?

DEREK. We haven't finished toasting Oliver.

JANE. (*Looks briefly at* OLIVER, *half-expecting him on a
barbecue spit.*) He looks all right to me . . . but listen,
the soup will get cold—

DEREK. Oh, have cook put it in the oven, or something.

JANE. (*Leaning away from kitchen, says in hoarse
whisper:*) I don't dare! She's just readying the individual
desserts for the oven!

OLIVER. What sort of desserts, Jane?

JANE. I believe it's baked alaska, sir.

WU. Baked alaska? . . . What is baked alaska?

GEORGE. (*As all others look toward* WU.) It's a sort of

combination thing—cake topped with ice cream, and then meringue over all of it, browned in the oven. . . . I think.

WU. Maid brings this now?

OLIVER. Hardly, Wu Chang. That is the dessert.

WU. Ah, the dessert! . . . Maid brings this now?

OLIVER. You don't understand—the dessert is always the last thing served.

WU. Why? . . . (*There is a pause, while all rack their brains, look at one another, and realize they don't know the answer.*)

OLIVER. Be-because—it wouldn't—uh—*be* dessert if it came first.

WU. What would it be?

DEREK. The—antipasto.

WU. What is antipasto tonight?

JANE. (*Curtsies.*) Cream of chicken soup, your highness, sir.

WU. Why do we not have soup for dessert, and baked alaska for antipasto?

OLIVER. Well—I suppose—? (*Looks around at others, all of whom shrug helplessly.*) I guess we *could.* . . . Jane, tell Mildred we'll have the dessert first.

JANE. *You* tell her.

OLIVER. I beg your pardon?

JANE. (*Draws herself up with dignity.*) Sir, I've worked for you for five years, now, and I know Mildred! After telling her five for dinner, then six, then seven, then making three calls for dinner while she tried not to burn the roast, and watching her assemble those baked alaskas, one by one, I'm not going out there to tell her you've decided to serve the dessert first!

OLIVER. Now, Jane, really!

JANE. I'm not *afraid* of her, mind you. Not the least bit. Not at all.

OLIVER. Then go tell Mildred we'll have the dessert first.

JANE. *You* tell her.

OLIVER. I thought you weren't afraid of her?

JANE. I'm not afraid of water, either—but I don't jump into it when it's boiling!

OLIVER. Jane, Mildred may become *upset*, but there is nothing to actually *fear!*

JANE. Then *you* tell her.

OLIVER. All right, damn it, I will! (*Jumps up and storms out into kitchen; everyone Onstage waits and listens; there is a silence; then from the kitchen comes a CRASH of cutlery, pots, pans, plates, etc., followed by a thunder of FOOTBALLS and the SLAM of a door; OLIVER re-enters, stops just within room; all eyes are on him; after a brief and uncomfortable moment, he clears his throat, then speaks.*) How about a *buffet* supper?

PEGGY. (*Rises, will start kitchenward on:*) Oh, don't be silly, Oliver. Here, you sit back down, and Jane and I will tend to everything. Come on, Jane. (*As he obediently re-sits, they exit to kitchen.*)

DEREK. (*Lifts water pitcher.*) Almost out of water!

OLIVER. I beg your pardon?

DEREK. This water-pitcher's nearly empty.

OLIVER. Nonsense, it's nearly three-quarters full.

DEREK. And it's already at room temperature.

OLIVER. With ice cubes in it?

DEREK. (*Rises, with pitcher.*) And there's a beetle in it.

SYLVIA. Picky-picky!

DEREK. (*Starts toward "hall."*) I think I'll refill it.

GEORGE. The water faucets are in the kitchen.

DEREK. The ice bucket is in the library.

J.D. The ice trays are in the refrigerator.

WU. (*Joining into the spirit of the thing.*) The hat of my aunt is on the table.

SYLVIA. (*Following his misdirected drift.*) I have lost my red pencil box.

OLIVER. (*Blankly, as others all chuckle.*) Is everybody nuts around here?

SYLVIA. (*As* DEREK *exits to "hall" with pitcher.*) All in favor say "aye."

WU. Where is baked alaska?

GEORGE. Peggy and Jane are bringing it.

WU. I think that I shall like it.

OLIVER. I hope so. It just cost me a cook.

WU. In mountains of Tibet, we have no cooks.

OLIVER. You do your own cooking?

WU. We cook nothing. We eat food as it is caught.

GEORGE. How can you catch anything when you sit around contemplating all day?

WU. When food comes close by, we catch it.

GEORGE. And if *no* food comes by?

WU. We contemplate a little harder.

J.D. Just what *do* you contemplate?

SYLVIA. (*With a what-*else? *shrug:*) Food!

(PEGGY *and* JANE *enter with trayful of individual baked alaskas; they move to* WU, JANE *holding tray while* PEGGY *hands out the plates—each plate having its dessert fork on it, of course, since the on-table cutlery is fastened down—and starting with* WU, *a dessert is put at each place, on:*)

PEGGY. For our guest of honor . . . and here's for George . . . Sylvia . . . one for Derek . . . one for myself . . . J.D. . . . and last but not least! (*Sets final dessert before* OLIVER *as* JANE *exits to kitchen with empty tray; sits at her own place, then all watch* WU *anxiously as he takes a tentative forkful and eats it; then:*) Well—? How do you like it?

WU. (*Thoughtfully.*) Top is hot . . . inside is cold . . . bottom is spongy and wet. It reminds me of . . . *life!*

OLIVER. Fascinating! Isn't it fascinating?

SYLVIA. Oh, yes, very. But—I don't get it.

GEORGE. Me, neither.

J.D. Could you explain it, please, Wu Chang?

WU. In the summer, all is dry and hot. That is top of baked alaska.

OLIVER. I told you he was marvelous! Go on, Wu Chang!

WU. In the winter, all nature is shrouded in bitter cold, but love can make the bitterness sweet. That is center of baked alaska.

SYLVIA. (*Caught up in the moment, offers tentatively:*) And the cake is dry and crumbly like autumn, and the melting ice cream is soggy and wet, like spring, April, time for romance—?

WU. (*Looks her up and down, then speaks.*) How would you like to become a monk?

OLIVER. In a Tibetan monastery, women are not allowed.

GEORGE. No wonder they sit and stare!

OLIVER. George, that's profane!

SYLVIA. (*Still muddled by it all.*) But Wu Chang—if summer, spring and the other seasons are locked into the baked alaska—I still don't see what it has to do with *life*. I mean, where do *people* get into the act?

WU. People eat the baked alaska.

GEORGE. That doesn't make sense.

OLIVER. It doesn't have to make sense! Wu Chang is a mystic!

(DEREK *re-enters with water pitcher;* WU *holds up emptied wine glass to him.*)

WU. I will have some of that.

DEREK. (*Oddly uneasy.*) What—? Oh, come now, you don't want any of this! I'll have Jane bring you more wine!

WU. My body is not accustomed to wine. I would prefer the water.

DEREK. But—this pitcher is from *our* end of the table—!

OLIVER. Stop babbling nonsense, Derek, and pour Wu Chang a drink of water!

J.D. (*Conversationally, as* DEREK *glumly fills* WU'S *glass.*) The way he hangs onto that pitcher, you'd think there was *gin* in it! (*All laugh but* DEREK *and* SYLVIA, who exchange looks of, respectively, despair and dawning comprehension.)

DEREK. (*As he finishes pouring.*) There you are, old man. Uh—sip it slowly—! (*Then stands there in horror as* WU *drains glass in one gulp; a moment later,* WU *quivers, blinks, and freezes in position.*)

OLIVER. (*Noticing none of this.*) You know, Wu Chang, I'm still a bit confused about the baked alaska . . . Wu Chang—? . . . Wu Chang—? (WU *sits silent, fist fast about stem of emptied glass.*)

DEREK. (*Trying to avert disaster.*) What are you confused *about?*

OLIVER. Oh, that's right, you missed it. See—meringue is summer, ice cream is winter, cake is fall, and drippings are spring. I don't get it.

DEREK. (*Honestly.*) Now *I'm* confused!

PEGGY. Baked alaska, Derek. Wu Chang says it reminds him of life.

DEREK. You mean it starts out fairly frothy, but after awhile it's not so hot?

SYLVIA. Bravo, Derek, that's one up on Wu!

GEORGE. (*Reaching for pitcher* DEREK *still holds.*) I give up. I'll settle for water. *That* I can understand—! (*Looks in surprise as* SYLVIA *restrains his reach.*) Hey, what is this, Indian wrestling?

SYLVIA. That's Wu's water!

DEREK. Right! After all, he's guest of honor!

OLIVER. (*Peering across table at* WU.) Wu Chang—is there anything wrong—?

WU. (*Shudders, blinks from frozen stasis, takes pitcher from* DEREK.) Oliver Stratton—whence comes this water?

OLIVER. From the faucet—no, wait, Derek, where *did* you get it? There are no faucets in the library.

DEREK. Uh. Melted ice. In the ice bucket. I filled it from that. Colder that way. Puts hair on your chest.

SYLVIA. *Now* he tells me!

WU. (*As* DEREK *sits in his place with reluctance and foreboding.*) Oliver Stratton—in Tibet, no such water as this exists.

OLIVER. Then what do you drink?

WU. Oh, there is water—but *this* magical liquid—drinking it—I am alive!

GEORGE. What were you *before* you drank it?

SYLVIA. Thirsty.

WU. This must be traced! Before the glass—the pitcher . . . before the pitcher—the ice . . . before the ice—?

PEGGY. You mean where did we get the water in the first place? I think it's from the river—after a lot of chemistry and filtration.

WU. Ah! Chemistry! That explains it! The people of New York are thrice blessed to dwell amid such wonderful technology! It quenches—and yet, it burns!

GEORGE. Now I *am* thirsty! (*Starts to reach for pitcher,* SYLVIA *grabs his arm again.*) Sylvia, do you *mind?!*

SYLVIA. Leave it alone! That's Wu's water!

GEORGE. Cut it out! (*Pulls free, gives her a shove, she slaps his hand.*)

OLIVER. (*Who looked their way too late.*) George? What's happening over there?

WU. The young lady smote the young gentleman.

OLIVER. Sylvia, why did you smite—uh—slap—George?

SYLVIA. Uh—there was a mosquito on his hand!

GEORGE. (*Looks at hand.*) Where?

SYLVIA. He got away.

DEREK. Say, Sylvia, I'm thirsty, would you pass me some of Wu's water?

SYLVIA. Sure thing! (*Jumps up, leans past* GEORGE, *grabs pitcher and hands it to* DEREK, *who immediately tries to pour some into* PEGGY'S *glass.*)

PEGGY. (*Preventing him.*) Derek, what are you doing?!

DEREK. The wine's very strong—I thought I'd *dilute* it a bit for you!

OLIVER. I thought *you* were thirsty—?

DEREK. Peggy's thirstier.

SYLVIA. I can see her lips cracking from here.

PEGGY. How can you see anything with those dark glasses on?

SYLVIA. I'm used to the dark.

GEORGE. That's what comes of dating Derek.

SYLVIA. You've never seen me on a date with Derek!

GEORGE. Nobody has. It's too dark.

OLIVER. What's that supposed to mean?

GEORGE. Don't ask questions. I'm a mystic.

WU. (*Dreamily.*) The Hudson is a marvelous river.

OLIVER. What makes you bring that up? (WU *suddenly hiccups.*)

GEORGE. What makes you bring *that* up?

PEGGY. Wait a minute—let me see that pitcher of water!

SYLVIA. On second thought, you don't look as thirsty as I thought. (PEGGY *gets grip on pitcher; they tug-of-war.*) Let go! You're going to spill it!

PEGGY. Give me that pitcher! Give it to me! *I* want a drink of that!

DEREK. (*To* OLIVER.) See? And this is only *water!* (*As* OLIVER *reacts,* SYLVIA *suddenly wrests pitcher free, loses balance, and dumps entire pitcher in* DEREK'S *lap; he sits quite still; then, after an exquisite pause:*) If you thought I needed a shower, you could have said so.

SYLVIA. (*Glumly sets pitcher on table.*) Well, unless anyone wants cold sandwiches, I'd say dinner was finished.

WU. Is there no after-dinner entertainment?

SYLVIA. Could be. If some kind soul will strike a match, perhaps Derek would do his famous imitation of a shrieking crepe suzette! (SANDERS *enters from "hall."*)

SANDERS. Mister Stratton, there is a person on the phone.

OLIVER. Person?

SANDERS. A lady, sir. She desires to bring you some literature.

OLIVER. I already have more books than I know what to do with.

SANDERS. I believe this literature is in the nature of a tract, sir. The woman is affiliated with some sort of temperance movement.

OLIVER. You mean she's a demon-rum prohibitionist?

SANDERS. That was my impression, sir.

OLIVER. Wonderful! And opportune! Tell her to come by at once! (*To* PEGGY, *as* SANDERS *exits.*) Some day you'll thank me, my dear. (*As she reacts blankly he continues to* WU.) That is—do we have *time* to see this woman, Wu Chang?

WU. If you have the Hudson, we have the time.

DEREK. (*Picks up pitcher, starts out.*) I'll get some more. But then I've got to change.

SYLVIA. Oh, Derek—don't ever change! Stay just as you are.

DEREK. (*Pauses short of exit to "hall."*) Debonair and charming—?

SYLVIA. All wet. (DEREK *scowls and exits.*)

WU. (*Dreamily rotating goblet.*) A man could really contemplate if he could sit beside the Hudson. Or dabble his feet in it. Or bathe in it.

SYLVIA. Or drown in it.

WU. How would you like to become a monk?

SYLVIA. Who knows? A little of that *Hudson* and I might get into the *spirit* of things.

OLIVER. How's that again?

SYLVIA. A play on words.

OLIVER. I don't follow it.

SYLVIA. Don't ask for explanations. I'm a mystic.

DEREK. (*Re-entering with freshly filled pitcher.*) Have some more Hudson, Wu.

WU. (*As* DEREK *refills his glass.*) Three thousand blessings upon you. (*Hiccups.*)

SYLVIA. Three thousand and one.

DEREK. Did I miss anything while I was gone?

SYLVIA. Me, I hope.

WU. (*Takes sip of drink as* DEREK *sits, then speaks to* OLIVER.) Ollie, old boy—let's start our own lamasery, on the banks of the Hudson!

J.D. (*Rises and moves toward* WU.) Oliver, we'd better get Wu to bed.

OLIVER. Bed? But what about our ship?

J.D. I don't think Wu is in any condition to sail.

SYLVIA. Too bad you're not flying. That he could do.

OLIVER. (*Rising, goes to assist* J.D. *with* WU.) I don't understand. What's happened to him?

J.D. Nothing he can't sleep off.

OLIVER. But all he had was some wine. Could it be that his austere life in the lamasery has ill-prepared him for the life of a Long-Islander?

DEREK. (*To* SYLVIA.) In plainer words, are we stuck with a looped lama?

SYLVIA. Well, while everyone takes a vote, I'm going to have me a roast beef sandwich! (*Starts toward kitchen.*) Garlic or not, here I come!

DEREK. (*Following her.*) Not a bad idea. I hope the gravy's still hot. (*They exit.*)

OLIVER. (*As he and* J.D. *assist* WU *toward "hall."*) Peggy, when that temperance woman arrives, I want you to give her your undivided attention.

PEGGY. *My* undivided attention? Oliver, are you sure *you* don't need her help?

GEORGE. Yes, Dad. I mean, Peggy's barely had one glass of wine.

OLIVER. Don't try to cover for her, son. I know you love her.

GEORGE. What? *Me?* In love with *Peggy?!*

PEGGY. (*Stung.*) Well, excuse *me, Mis*-ter Stratton! (*Exits to kitchen.*)

J.D. Come on, Oliver, this monk is heavy!

GEORGE. Just a moment! Where did you get this nutty notion about Peggy?

OLIVER. A blind man could see you're crazy about her.

GEORGE. I mean about her needing a *temperance* lecture!

OLIVER. Why—from Derek and Sylvia.

GEORGE. And you *believed* them?

OLIVER. I can't think of a reason why they'd make such a thing up.

'GEORGE. I can think of forty million reasons! Don't you see? They want you to cut her out as beneficiary!

OLIVER. What?! But how did they know she *was* the beneficiary?

J.D. Uh—I'm afraid *I* may have let it slip . . . (*Almost drops* WU.) Like that.

OLIVER. But it was supposed to be a secret!

GEORGE. Well, it's all over the house, Dad.

OLIVER. Say, do you know you've called me "Dad" more times this evening than you ever did before in your life?

GEORGE. Well—I—I suppose it's sophisticated for kids in the "best" families to use first names—but—well, you're leaving, and—all at once, I wanted you to remember my calling you "Dad," instead of "Oliver."

OLIVER. Why, son. I'm touched. You've made me very happy.

GEORGE. I'm glad, Dad. And as for that beneficiary thing— (DEREK, SYLVIA *and* PEGGY *enter with sandwiches.*) Do as you like. Leave the money to us, or leave it to Peggy. It doesn't make any difference.

DEREK. Not to *you*, naturally!

GEORGE. (*Icily*.) And just what is *that* supposed to mean?

DEREK. Isn't it obvious? If he leaves it to *you*, you *get* it. If he leaves it to *Peggy*, you *marry* her and get it. (*To* OLIVER.) If you were leaving it to Sylvia, I could be every bit as noble as George.

PEGGY. And what makes you think *George* has a chance of marrying me? He doesn't even *love* me!

GEORGE. I didn't *say* that!

PEGGY. Then you *do* love me?

GEORGE. I didn't say *that*, either.

DEREK. Oh, good, it's still open season!

SYLVIA. I was afraid of that!

J.D. Afraid of what?

SYLVIA. You didn't see Derek's hotblooded session on the sofa with Little Miss Hygeine!

DEREK. Sylvia, I love no one but you.

SYLVIA. Derek, do you mean it? Why didn't you tell me?

DEREK. Until tonight, I never saw you with the lights on.

SYLVIA. Well, I guess I can vouch for that!

OLIVER. Enough of this squabbling! I am leaving my money to Peggy, and the rest of you can do what you like about it!

PEGGY. Oh, Oliver, how can you be so uncaring about your own flesh and blood!

OLIVER. Well, if that's all the thanks I get for my generosity, you can put down that sandwich and get out of my house!

GEORGE. If Peggy goes, I go!

DEREK. I'll call a cab.

OLIVER. *SILENCE!* (*He gets it.*) J.D.—take Wu Chang upstairs. He's not very large; you can make it.

J.D. (*Struggling Off Left with* WU.) Sanders! Sanders, are you out there? Give me a hand! (*From Off Left, we hear loud CLAPPING.*) Not like *that*, you idiot! (*Exits with* WU *barely stumbling along beside her.*)

OLIVER. (*Points after them, but while facing group.*)

Now, listen, all of you—maybe I'm a fool, but—Wu Chang is a very wise man. When he has awakened from his slumber, I intend to ask *him* to whom I should leave my money. I'm sure he will give a most learned answer.

SYLVIA. (*Dryly.*) Act Two: The Emerald City of Tibet!

OLIVER. Nonsense. Wu Chang is dedicated to higher things than money. I shall ask him, and I shall abide by his decision. Good evening, all of you. (*Exits Left.*)

PEGGY. Well—back to the clinic, I guess.

GEORGE. I'm going with you.

DEREK. Can you roll bandages?

SYLVIA. Oh, shut up, all of you. We've got to figure out what to do, and quickly! If we keep up this squabbling, we'll *all* be rolling bandages! United, we have a fighting chance. What do you say? A fourth of forty million is still better than unemployment compensation!

DEREK. True, but—united to do what? Wait till midnight, tie handkerchiefs over our faces, and machine-gun Oliver in his bed?

GEORGE. He's not *going* to bed. He's sailing, remember?

DEREK. (*Shrugs.*) Okay, so what's Plan *B?*

PEGGY. (*Giving it all up.*) Let me know if you think of one. *I'm* going to get a drink of water—*real* water!

GEORGE. (*Stops her before she can exit toward kitchen.*) Wait, Peggy. Derek's right. We must come up with a plan.

PEGGY. Well, look—it seems to me that, if Oliver is going to make his decision after he talks to *Wu Chang*—

SYLVIA. We influence *him!* Of course!

DEREK. Yes, but how? What kind of motivation moves a monk?

GEORGE. Sex!

SYLVIA. But monks have sworn *off* sex!

PEGGY. But it *must* still *appeal* to them! Look at how interested Wu Chang seemed to be in Sylvia—!

SYLVIA. Only as a new recruit. How could I spend the money if I wound up on some mountain-top with a rice bowl and a shaven head?!

DEREK. *You'd* find a way.

SYLVIA. *(Turns on him.)* I've had just enough of your innuendoes, Derek! *(Takes a roundhouse swing at him.)*

DEREK. *(Grabbing her arm.)* Hey, watch it—!

GEORGE. *(Grappling with DEREK.)* You're breaking her arm!

PEGGY. *(Grappling with GEORGE.)* George, this is no time to get physical!

DEREK. You mind your own business, you—hired girl!

GEORGE. You can't talk to Peggy like that!

SYLVIA. *(Writhing in DEREK's grip.)* Derek, the bone is starting to splinter—!

GEORGE. Let her go!

PEGGY. George, you're becoming emotional!

(And as all four wrestle, ad-libbing grunts and various imprecations, JANE enters from kitchen with soup.)

JANE. Doesn't anyone want dessert—? *(But by now the quartet is out of sight behind the table, from which point we hear screams, shouts and cries, and see an occasional flailing arm, flying shoe, etc., popping up into view; JANE calmly sits at Right end of table and begins sipping at a bowl of soup herself, on:)* Well, no use letting it go to waste . . . ! *(And as she sips serenely, and the free-for-all gets louder and louder—)*

The Curtain Falls

ACT TWO

Scene 1

The library, looking as we last saw it, just a short time later. SYLVIA, DEREK, PEGGY *and* GEORGE *are all seated side by side on the sofa, facing out front; all have elbows on knees, fists on chins. Until otherwise indicated, they remain in this position, not even looking toward one another as they speak, all lines directed out front. A few seconds after curtain-rise,* PEGGY *sighs, and:*

DEREK. Was that despair, exhaustion or self-pity?

PEGGY. Approximately one-third of each.

SYLVIA. If only we had the combination to the safe.

GEORGE. Are you suggesting we simply *take* the money? That's sheer thievery.

DEREK. You mean "efficiency."

PEGGY. Sounds more like larceny.

SYLVIA. Or just plain ingenuity.

DEREK. Why don't we hire ourselves out as a thesaurus?

GEORGE. Why don't we all shut up until we find a solution to our problem?

SYLVIA. It could get awfully quiet in here.

DEREK. We'd wind up covered with cobwebs.

(*As their morose dialogue continues,* JANE *and* SANDERS *enter, carrying a large tool box, and move to picture.*)

GEORGE. You know, there's a secret way to open the picture over the safe, but only my father knows it.

SYLVIA. Are you sure? Maybe Jane found the button while dusting, or something. (JANE *presses section of library shelf, and picture slides up to expose safe.*)

DEREK. I doubt it. Jane never dusts that thoroughly. (SANDERS *starts whacking safe door via hammer and chisel.*)

PEGGY. The radiators are knocking again.

DEREK. Enjoy the heat while you can. We'll all soon be out in the cold.

SYLVIA. Whatever possessed Oliver, turning every last asset into cash?

GEORGE. He said he hated legal fuss—inheritance taxes, stuff like that.

PEGGY. How could he *avoid* it?

GEORGE. Culver names the lucky winner—I mean, the heir—at the reading of the will, and then hands over the cash on the spot.

SYLVIA. (*Quietly awed.*) Forty million smackers . . . !

DEREK. He closed ten banks, withdrawing all that loot.

PEGGY. Say—aren't those radiators *unusually* noisy—?

(*But* SANDERS *at this moment, with a shrug at* JANE, *gives up, replaces hammer and chisel in tool box,* JANE *lowers the picture into place, and they cross and exit to hall, completing their exit on* DEREK'S *line, below:*)

GEORGE. Funny—I never heard them quite so loud *before* . . . ? (*Sits up straight, but still facing out front.*)

SYLVIA. Funny—I never *saw* any radiators *in* this room, before . . . ? (*Does same.*)

PEGGY. Even funnier—*I* never saw radiators anywhere in the *house*, before . . . ? (*Does same.*)

DEREK. *Hey*—this house is heated *electrically!* (*Does same.*)

ALL FOUR. Then what was that noise?!

(*All stand, look around left and right, up and down—then shrug in bemused puzzlement and seat themselves again, but no longer in pensive stances.*)

GEORGE. Probably the walls settling, or something. This is an old house.

PEGGY. I assumed as much—I mean, the Strattons have lived here for six generations.

DEREK. Of course, each generation has added some improvements—making things better and better—

SYLVIA. Until *you* were born!

GEORGE. Hold it! Let's not get another battle started. We've got to think of a way to get our rightful money.

PEGGY. Actually, it's yours and Derek's—Sylvia and I have no real claim.

SYLVIA. Speak for yourself, Nurse!

DEREK. What claim *do* you have, Sylvia, when you get right down to it . . . ?

SYLVIA. You claim the money, then I claim you.

PEGGY. That's getting *down* to it, all right!

SYLVIA. Drink has certainly sharpened that antiseptic little tongue!

PEGGY. It wasn't *my* idea to have so much wine!

SYLVIA. I didn't see anyone twisting your arm.

PEGGY. Then you weren't watching your boy friend!

SYLVIA. Naturally not! I *trust* him! And some day, rich or poor, I will count myself the luckiest girl in the world when he carries me across the threshold!

PEGGY. (*To* GEORGE.) Good thing she's planning to marry a *Derek!*

SYLVIA. I don't imagine *you* fit into a Size-Sixteen Maidenform!

PEGGY. Are you implying I'm overweight?!

SYLVIA. If the girdle fits, wear it! (*The women face one another, eyes ablaze.*)

GEORGE. Now *stop* it, both of you! This kind of in-fighting won't get us any richer. (*They subside, still seething a bit.*)

DEREK. George is right. Let's forget our petty differences, and *think!* (*All face front, bend forward, and*

*assume   that   elbows-on-knees-and-chins-on-fists   stance
again.)*
GEORGE. Now, let's all close our eyes and concentrate.
Don't let *anything* disturb us until we *think* of something!

*(All shut eyes tightly; while thus bemused, they do not
notice J.D. enter from hall, and she does not notice
any of them, either; she seems distraught, aggravated,
and she begins pacing impatiently, midway between
sofa and back wall; then WU enters from hall and
bows.)*

WU. A thousand blessings upon you.
J.D. Oh, cut it out, Charlie!
WU. *(Straightens, abruptly un-monklike, tosses back
hood and yawns delicately, scratching one side.)* Okay,
okay. Just wanted to keep in character in case somebody
else was hanging around. How'm I doing, so far?
J.D.   Lousy! . . . That   exhibition   at   dinner—!
"Whence comes this water?"! Ha! You knew damned well
it was gin!
WU. I was thirsty.
J.D. You almost blew the whole deal, you imbecile! And
your attitude toward Miss Crane—! "How would you like
to become a monk?"!
WU. *(Shrugs.)* I just tried to say what I figured a *real*
lama would say in the same situation—!
J.D. *(Disparagingly.)* Real Lama! How would *you*
know? You've never been east of Montauk Point!
WU. *(Defensively.)* Nobody caught *on*, did they?!
J.D. That's just dumb luck! If you stick to our plan,
everything will still work out—but you've got to get Oliver
out of here *tonight!*
WU. Hell, why don't I just *plug* him, boss?!
J.D. That's too easy. This must be *poetic* justice, or none
at all!

Wu. But boss—!

J.D. (*With shushing wave of hands.*) Quiet! I hear someone coming!

(Wu *replaces hood on head, tucks each hand into cuff of opposite sleeve,* J.D. *rushes to desk, sits, looks casual as possible, and then* OLIVER *enters from hall.*)

OLIVER. Wu Chang! I don't know you'd awakened already!

Wu. This humble one's person is much improved, thank you. Therefore, are you now ready to depart from this world, Oliver Stratton? (*As* OLIVER *and* J.D. *react.*) That is—from this materialistic Western World—? (*They recover.*)

OLIVER. Soon, very soon. But first I must see that temperance person, and get Miss Brent off the road to Whoopeeville!

Wu. She looked pretty good to *me*—! (*By reflex, gives appreciative whistle; then, when* OLIVER *and* J.D. *react, covers with:*) That is the song of Himalayan Nightingale. Always played for nurses.

OLIVER. There are birds at the lamasery? I thought it was far too high.

J.D. (*Stands, extemporizes quickly.*) Oh, it is—that is, they can't live without help. That's why the lamasery was built, to help the birds survive the height—you know, water, seeds, nesting holes—

OLIVER. I had no idea! Wu Chang, is that a fact?

Wu. (*With solemn nod.*) Lamasery is for the birds, all right— (*They react again.*) Uh—I mean, our major activity is building shelters for—uh—for tired condors!

OLIVER. Condors? Condors in Tibet? I thought they came from Peru?

J.D./Wu. That's why they're so *tired*—! (*Then they glare at one another, during:*)

OLIVER. (*Nods thoughtfully.*) That makes sense.

J.D. (*Relieved.*) I'm glad you think so! Would anyone like a brandy? *I* sure would!

WU. (*Enthused, rubs hands.*) Yeah, I could *use* a little hair of the dog—I mean—of the Abominable Snowman!

OLIVER. I thought that was a legend! Have you *seen* the Abominable Snowman?

WU. Uh—only a glimpse—at a distance—but it always runs away!

OLIVER. Can't anybody *catch* it?

J.D. What would they *do* with it?

WU. And why would they *want* it?

DEREK. (*Snaps out of concentration, jumps to his feet.*) I've *got* it! (*As co-conspirators sit up.*)

OLIVER. (*As* WU *and* J.D. *react in shock.*) *Where?!* (*Then, as* DEREK *reacts to his voice, he reacts to* DEREK.) Derek! Have you been here all along?

DEREK. Well, not since the dawn of time, exactly—but a reasonable amount of time—

J.D. You mean, while *I* was talking to *Wu—?!*

DEREK. (*Blank.*) For all I know. Why, did I miss something important?

WU. Not a thing! We didn't say a word!

PEGGY. Then how were you talking?

WU. Uh . . . *sign language!* (*Quickly turns to* J.D., *makes elaborate hand-moves during:*)

J.D. (*As if reading them.*) My! . . . You don't say! . . . Not really! . . . How interesting! . . .

OLIVER. J.D.—you never told me you knew sign language.

J.D. You never asked me.

OLIVER. Could Wu teach *me?*

WU. Later, at the lamasery.

J.D. Good idea! Well, *bon voyage,* you two!

OLIVER. I can't leave yet. Peggy must be put on the road to sobriety!

J.D. Nonsense! She's just fine! She looks absolutely marvelous!

WU. Practically terrific! (*Whistles again.*)

GEORGE. What was that—?

OLIVER. (*Informatively.*) A tired condor.

SYLVIA. A *what*? (*Then reacts to* PEGGY, *who had risen and is now trying to "sneak" a bottle into the bosom of her dress.*) Peggy, what are you doing?

PEGGY. Nothing! Pay no attention! Where liquor's concerned, I can take it or leave it alone! . . . Right now, I'm taking it!

OLIVER. Well, leave it alone!

PEGGY. (*Avoiding his grasp, hams it up good.*) No! Don't touch it! I want it! I must have it! I need it!

GEORGE. Peggy!

PEGGY. Oh, you don't know what it's like, being without it! First the hot and cold flashes—then the icy sweats—then, one by one, bats—bats—*bats*—!

OLIVER. Really?!

PEGGY. (*As if it were an explanation.*) I hate to drink alone.

OLIVER. Oh, the poor child!

GEORGE. (*Seeing an advantage.*) If she's *poor*, whose fault *is* it?!

PEGGY. Poverty makes me thirsty.

OLIVER. All right, all right—I'll leave the money to Miss Brent!

DEREK. What about Sylvia? She's even a worse lush than Peggy!

SYLVIA. (*Grabbing this cue, sinks dramatically back onto sofa.*) Oh, Derek, to have my secret shame just blurted out like that! I can never face anyone again! (*Covers face.*)

OLIVER. (*Moves toward her.*) Oh, my dear! Yes, you can—!

PEGGY. (*Trying to get the ball back on her side of the court.*) Aaaagh! They're crawling all over me—down my forehead—down my face—down my throat—down my—uh— (*Looks uncertainly into bosom.*)

WU. (*Enthusiastically.*) Don't stop *now!* (*When* OTHERS *stare.*) I mean—keep fighting them! *Brush*—brush like *anything!*

PEGGY. (*Resumes brushing.*) Aaagh! Bats! Aaaagh! Spiders! Aaaagh! . . . Uh—?

GEORGE. (*Helpfully, points toward her chest.*) Centipedes!

OLIVER. *You* can see them?

GEORGE. Well, *I* enjoy a little nip *myself!*

WU. (*Moves gleefully toward* PEGGY.) Here, let me help you brush! (*But* J.D. *grabs him by the arm, holds him back.*)

SYLVIA. (*Fighting for* OLIVER's *attention, still on sofa.*) Oh, the agony—the remorse—the shame—the scandal! And despite my unhappiness, Oliver walks away from me!

OLIVER. (*Turns, starts toward her.*) My dear, I didn't mean to—

PEGGY. An elephant! My very first! A whole *herd* of elephants! Look at them, every color of the rainbow! Hi, there, Jumbo! Hi, there, all of you!

OLIVER. (*Will react, and turn her way.*) Good heavens! (*Over next 14 lines, he will look toward one speaker, then the other, not knowing which way to move:*)

SYLVIA. I feel so despicable—so loathsome—so repulsive—!

PEGGY. Snakes! Fighting with the elephants!

SYLVIA. I've hit the bottom—there's no way up—!

PEGGY. Fang against tusk! It's colossal! Bite, thrust, hiss, trumpet, wiggle, waddle—!

SYLVIA. Oh, the sorrow of a secret shame made known to the world—!

PEGGY. The bats are back! In technicolor!

SYLVIA. Agony! Sorrow! Shame!

PEGGY. Fight—fight—fight!

SYLVIA. The humiliation of it all—!

PEGGY. Down, boy! Easy there—!

SYLVIA. (*Louder.*) Degradation!

PEGGY. (*Louder.*) A menagerie!

SYLVIA. I'll be in the National Enquirer!

PEGGY. I'll be in Bellevue!

OLIVER. I'll be a monkey's uncle!

DEREK. I resent that!

J.D. (*Desperately.*) Please, please, everybody! (*All look her way.*) Oliver will miss his boat!

OLIVER. Drat, he's right! After all, Wu Chang came half-way around the world to get me—the least I can do is be punctual.

J.D. Good thinking! Go! Now! I'll handle this domestic crisis.

WU. Come, Oliver Stratton. The boat awaits our boarding!

OLIVER. But that temperance person—?

J.D. I'll be glad to welcome her in your stead.

OLIVER. Oh—very well, very well! Let's go, Wu Chang. (*Exits to hall with* WU.)

PEGGY. (*Sets bottle back on table as others slump.*) Well, *that* was a sobering experience!

J.D. Nice try, all of you. I'll just see Oliver off! (*Exits to hall.*)

SYLVIA. Wait! I've got it! Oliver can't sail if he doesn't have a *ticket—!*

DEREK. A beautiful idea! I'll phone right now and cancel! (*Starts toward desk.*)

GEORGE. No! J.D. will be back, and stop you! Use the upstairs extension!

PEGGY. And hurry!

DEREK. Gotcha! (*Rushes out into hall;* PEGGY *sits on sofa with* GEORGE *and* SYLVIA; *all lean back, slumped low, thinking; as they do,* SANDERS *and* JANE *enter from hall; he carries an electric drill, the cord trailing after him;* JANE *once more raises picture, then plugs cord into outlet, and* SANDERS *starts drilling at safe, in short bursts.*)

SYLVIA. The mosquitoes are *noisy* tonight!

GEORGE. Never mind the mosquitoes, *think!* Even if Derek cancels the ticket, there'll be other boats. Delaying his departure doesn't *solve* anything, it just gives us more *time!*

PEGGY. Time to what? That drunken-bit didn't work, for either of us!

SYLVIA. Maybe united thinking *isn't* the answer! What if we all split up, came up with schemes of our own—maybe *one* of us would hit the Stratton jackpot—!

GEORGE. And where would that leave the *others?*

SYLVIA. (*Shrugs.*) With a very rich friend who *wasn't* going to Tibet!

PEGGY. Good point, Sylvia, good point!

GEORGE. Mmm, I don't know—I prefer teamwork!

PEGGY. Can't cut it *alone,* huh?

GEORGE. That's a lousy thing to say! And speaking of lousy things—where did this money-mad nature of yours emerge from, anyhow?!

PEGGY. You think I'm plotting for myself?! You numbskull, I'm doing this for *you!*

GEORGE. To save my rightful inheritance?! Oh, Peggy—darling—is this true?

PEGGY. (*After a pause.*) Hell, no! It's for me, all right! After all, Oliver *planned* to leave me the loot until Derek and this Bronx Buttinski chimed in! I'm just being fair to Oliver's wishes.

SYLVIA. Such selfless devotion is touching.

PEGGY. Don't preach to *me* about selflessness! Not the way you and Derek have been meshing gears all night! I have as much right as *anybody* to swing the money my way—and *more* right than *some* people—! (*Pauses, sniffs the air.*) I smell hot metal!

SYLVIA. Come to think of it—so do I—! (SANDERS *and* JANE *will give up, as before, lower picture, and exit with drill to hall, during:*)

GEORGE. Can't be! We've already established we have no radiators!

SYLVIA. Then what could it possibly be *from*—?!

(*The* TRIO *stands, looking left and right, up and down, very puzzled; then* DEREK *rushes in from hall.*)

DEREK. There's no ticket for Uncle Oliver!

GEORGE. Good work, Derek!

DEREK. No-no, you don't understand! There never *was* one!

PEGGY. But—there must have been!

DEREK. I know, but—when I called to cancel, they said they never heard of him—or Wu Chang, either!

PEGGY. How strange!

SYLVIA. Yes, but how lucky!

GEORGE. Lucky or not, there's something extremely odd about it! (*Then all look up as* OLIVER, WU *and* J.D. *enter from hall.*)

OLIVER. The taxi's here. Just thought I'd say goodbye, before we sail for the mysterious East—!

GEORGE. It's more mysterious than you think.

SYLVIA. Just what do you and Wu plan to sail *on?*

PEGGY. Unless you'll both fit on top of Oliver's steamer trunk!

DEREK. And it's seaworthy!

OLIVER. What do you mean?

SYLVIA. Only that Derek phoned the steamship company to—uh—*confirm* your reservation—and they don't *have* one!

OLIVER. J.D.! I thought *you* made that reservation!

J.D. Wu Chang! I thought *you* made it!

WU. Oliver Stratton, I thought *you* made it!

OLIVER. (*Shrugs.*) Ah, well, these things happen. J.D.— get on the phone and make us a reservation on the next ship out. Meantime, Wu Chang, you must remain here as my guest. I hope I can make things austere enough for you.

Wu. Oh, don't bother! For the time being, I don't mind putting up with luxury.

OLIVER. Nonsense, I wouldn't hear of it! I'll have Sanders take all the liquor, magazines and even the innerspring mattress out of the guest room, so you can feel at home.

Wu. *Please*, Oliver Stratton—let me *suffer* a little!

OLIVER. Don't be silly. Never let it be said that Oliver Stratton doesn't cater to his guests. I'll have Sanders nail the windows open and turn off the heat, too, so you can truly feel you're back in the windswept mountains of Tibet!

Wu. (*Slumps, aghast, but murmurs.*) Words fail me— you—you—wonderful person! (*To* J.D.) Make haste to arrange passage for us, lest I be killed with kindness!

J.D. Soon as I send the taxi away. (*Exits to hall;* OLIVER *and* WU *head that way.*)

OLIVER. Well, guess I'll be going to bed—unless someone feels like playing a little gin rummy—?

DEREK. For money?

OLIVER. Afraid my money's all in that safe. How about toothpicks?

DEREK. No thanks. When you're starving, who needs 'em?!

OLIVER. Well, then, I'll say goodnight! (*Exits, followed by* WU.)

PEGGY. Well, *I'm* going upstairs and make my *own* plan. Time is running out!

GEORGE. Peggy's right. Couples do better if they stay apart. I'm going to my room. Come on, Peggy!

PEGGY. (*As he arm-tugs her along.*) To your *room?* Why, George, how romantic—! Or *is* it? (*They exit.*)

SYLVIA. You Strattons are all alike.

DEREK. When it comes to money, everybody's alike! (*Similarly tugs her hallward.*) I, too, have a room! We'll go there, and sit, and plot, and—!

SYLVIA. And you may end up with a black eye of your own!

(*But she exits with him; a moment later,* SANDERS *and* JANE
*enter from garden; he carries a manual insect-spray-
gun;* JANE *raises picture as before.*)

SANDERS. Are you sure muriatic acid will affect solid
steel? (*Starts spritzing face of safe.*) It'd be much simpler to
tie Mister Stratton down and torture the combination out of
him.

JANE. I hate the sight of blood, Herbert.

SANDERS. I'd be glad to lend you a blindfold. (*Still spritzing.*) Listen, you'd better go out in the hall and signal me if
you see anyone coming. Can you whistle "Yankee
Doodle"?

JANE. No . . . but I can *sing* it—?

SANDERS. It's better than nothing. (*Continues spritzing
as she exits; then:*)

JANE. (*Off. Sings.*) "Yankee Doodle went to town, riding on a pony, stuck a feather in his cap—" (SANDERS, *of
course, has instantly lowered picture and fled with sprayer
to garden; on final bit of song,* JANE *backs into room,
followed by a puzzled* DEREK:) "—and called it *Derek
Stratton* . . . !"

DEREK. Lovely, Jane, just lovely. I'll drop a note to the
Mormon Tabernacle Choir in the morning.

SYLVIA. (*Enters behind him.*) Derek, what was that awful
racket?

JANE. I was singing.

DEREK. Yes, but why?

JANE. (*Shrugs.*) Why *not?!* (*Then, as* DEREK *and* SYLVIA
sit on sofa.) Sir— (*Gives an anxious glance gardenward.*)
Do you—intend to *sit* there, on that sofa—?!

DEREK. Unless you'd prefer I did a handstand.

SYLVIA. In *your* condition?

DEREK. (*Goes to retort, then senses* JANE *is still there,
turns.*) Uh—Jane—if you're waiting to *see* that
handstand—

JANE. What? Oh—uh—no, sir. Sorry, sir. (*Exits to hall, after one more worried gardenward glance; even as* DEREK *turns to speak to* SYLVIA, SANDERS *enters from garden, tiptoes toward safe, carrying that toolbox again;* JANE *immediately steps in from hall, stands at attention just inside room, and sings:*) "Yankee Doodle went to town, riding on a—!"

DEREK. (*Jumps up, waving his arms frenziedly at her.*) In the *morning*, Jane, I'll write in the *morning—! (Startled,* SANDERS *drops toolbox with a loud crash;* SYLVIA *jumps to her feet to stare at him, as:*) Sanders, will you please get those tools out of here and stop all these constant interruptions?! (SANDERS *flees to hall with toolbox,* JANE *following;* DEREK, *annoyed, sits again, and so does* SYLVIA, *on:*) A man can't have any peace in his own home, with that kind of—of— (*Pauses, puzzled.*) *Tools?*

SYLVIA. Darling, you look so odd—*shouldn't* he be carrying tools?

DEREK. A *butler?!*

SYLVIA. Never having had one of my own, I can't be held responsible for having a rather dim knowledge of their duties. I thought he might be fixing the plumbing, or something.

DEREK. Sylvia, if you don't like our plumbing, you know what you can do!

SYLVIA. Yes, but *where?!*

DEREK. That was unworthy of you, Sylvia. Come, help me think this thing out . . . Why would Sanders have a bunch of tools?

SYLVIA. You don't suppose he was trying to crack the safe?

DEREK. Impossible. Only Uncle Oliver even knows where it's *at!*

SYLVIA. Then I guess we'll never know. It'll be one of life's mysteries, like those strange little stories in the Sunday supplements.

DEREK. (*Brightens, starts toward bookshelves.*) You know, you've given me an idea. I wonder if we have any good informative material on Tibet—?

SYLVIA. (*Trailing after him.*) You still think there's something funny going on, and you want to stop it, huh?

DEREK. Or get *in* on it! (*Moves along bookshelves, scanning titles, opens a book.*) Ah, an encyclopedia! Maybe there's something *here* . . . let's see . . . *Tarantulas* . . . *Terpsichore* . . . *Thermometers* . . . *Tia Juana* . . . !

SYLVIA. *Tibet*—! (*Tries to grab book before he does, and somehow the secret button is activated, and the picture slides up.*) Derek—look!

DEREK. The safe! With forty million dollars in it—just inches away.

SYLVIA. But those inches are made of solid steel!

DEREK. There must be a way in, somehow! There's got to be!

SYLVIA. And if you *do* get the money—then what?

DEREK. You mean—*us?* (*When she nods unhappily, he takes her hands.*) Sylvia, darling, if you'll help me get into that safe tonight, I will gladly become Mister Sylvia Crane tomorrow morning!

SYLVIA. Oh, Derek—if I thought you meant that—I'd hock my watch, buy a stick of TNT—

DEREK. And have the entire household on our necks! . . . Possibly the entire *house!* No, darling, don't fret. Derek has a plan.

SYLVIA. Who gets the gin *this* time?

DEREK. Sylvia, I'm being brilliant, don't interfere with me!

SYLVIA. —said the cigarette on its way into the cuspidor!

DEREK. Stop being so pessimistic and pay attention! We may not be able to get into the *safe*—but we *can* get into Oliver's heart!

SYLVIA. With a dumdum bullet?

DEREK. Better than that—with *pathos*, darling. Oliver would never think of leaving a lady in distress. (*Portentously.*) Sylvia—you are going to have a baby!

SYLVIA. Impossible! I haven't even knitted the little booties!

DEREK. Cut it out, and listen! We can't just rush up to Oliver and *tell* him your condition—he might suspect it's a lie. We must work it so that he thinks he's discovered something we've been *keeping* from him! Our approach must be devious—subtle—

SYLVIA. How about I rush up to him and scream, "A pickle! I must have a pickle!"?

DEREK. Much too crude. We want to hint, not spell it out in neon. . . . Hmm . . . what you said before gives me an idea—*can* you *knit* a bootie?

SYLVIA. Just *one?* What kind of baby *is* this?

DEREK. All right, skip it. Maybe there's a better way—

SYLVIA. I could go into labor on the sofa.

DEREK. Darling, labor must produce something besides loud shrieks, when Oliver's expecting a baby!

SYLVIA. He's pregnant, too?

DEREK. Now, listen—!

SYLVIA. Okay-okay. Let me get this thing straight. I assume that *you* are to be considered the *sire* of this one-bootie child?

DEREK. Naturally. I mean, my uncle can't contribute to the support of just *anybody*'s baby!

SYLVIA. What makes you think he'll contribute to *this* one's? He might just say "Congratulations!" and sail out of our lives!

DEREK. But how would his grand-nephew be supported?

SYLVIA. You could get a job . . . ?

DEREK. Bite your tongue! . . . But, I must admit, you have a point. Still, there must be some way to make him want to— (*Snaps fingers, inspired.*) Sylvia! I've got it! *I'm a cad!*

SYLVIA. So what else is new?

DEREK. (*Patiently.*) I mean I *play* a cad, a no-good heel, in our turgid little drama. Imagine the effect on Oliver if he hears me refusing to marry you—laughing at you—scorning you—sneering—scoffing—jibing—!

SYLVIA. Don't *I* get any dialogue?

DEREK. Mostly sobs. Maybe all sobs. Bitter weeping and tooth-gnashing.

SYLVIA. How do you gnash one tooth?

DEREK. Sylvia—!

SYLVIA. Sorry. But, be reasonable: If I don't have any lines, how do I spill the beans about my condition? After all, Oliver has to know what you're being a cad *about!*

DEREK. Hmm. You're right. (*Starts for desk.*) Close that panel and come with me. (*As* SYLVIA *locates and presses button, he takes up pencil and paper, sits at desk.*) I think this is going to require a little scripting. Let's see—you can be seated on the *sofa* when he comes in, and I— No, wait. *I* will be seated there, and you will be on your *knees* before me, begging—pleading—! No, wait. *I* will be standing over there, looking out into the garden, and you will be *lying on the floor* at my heels, piteous, distraught, desperate—!

SYLVIA. Hey, one more change of blocking and I'll be in the *cellar!* Derek, *must* I be the wailing type? I see myself a bit more self-controlled; sad, but with a reserve of icy dignity. I plead—but with pride. I beg, but with calm. I implore, but with aplomb—!

DEREK. Yes! That's it! (*Starts scribbling.*) With reserve . . . with dignity . . . with pride . . . with calm . . . with aplomb—!

SYLVIA. And don't forget "with *child*," or the whole thing's a waste of time.

DEREK. Got it. Now, here are our lines . . . (*She leans over his shoulder, watching him write.*) I say— (*Scribbles and scribbles.*) Then *you* say— (*Writes barely a word.*) Then *I* say— (*Scribbles and scribbles.*)

SYLVIA. Hold it! Where's *my* share of this exposition?! I have less dialogue than Buster Keaton! I must be able to think of *something* to say besides, "But, Derek—!"

DEREK. All right, all right! You say *this* . . . then I'll say *that* . . . then you say *this* . . . then I'll say *that* . . . *! (He has been writing frantically, but now he stops, and* SYLVIA *turns, as* GEORGE *and* PEGGY *enter from hall.)*

PEGGY. Hi! What are *you* two up to?

SYLVIA. This and that.

DEREK. *(Stands with script.)* Wait'll you hear our plan!

GEORGE. No, thanks, we have one of our own.

DEREK. Not as good as ours, I'll bet!

GEORGE. Oh, yes! We've been really clever. You see, we decided that—

DEREK. But *we* came up with the original notion that—

SYLVIA/PEGGY. *(Completing the phrase gleefully.)* —*I'm* going to have a *baby!*

(Then each reacts as if the other's words were true, and they rush into each other's arms, ad-libbing squeals of congratulation, while GEORGE *and* DEREK *each pump the other's hand, slap each other on the back, and then:)*

DEREK. *(Realizes.)* Hey—you mean—a make-believe baby? Like *ours?*

SYLVIA. *Theirs* probably has *two* booties.

GEORGE. But—we can't *both* couples have babies—can we?

DEREK. It's—stretching things—even for Uncle Oliver . . .

PEGGY. I've got it! Sylvia can have the baby—I'll have the fatal disease!

SYLVIA. You mean—one giving life—one losing it—?

GEORGE. But what kind of disease?

PEGGY. Oh, I know all kinds—jungle rot, snakebite, ptomaine, fadeaway—

DEREK. What's fadeaway?

PEGGY. An opera disease. The lady gets weak, gets pale, and gets sexier and sexier as the disease progresses. No annoying sneezing, or vomiting and diarrhea—

SYLVIA. Okay, we *get* it, we *get* it! . . . But—which of us gets what?

DEREK. I'll flip a coin. Heads you have a baby—tails you fade away—! (*Flips coin, all look at it and gasp with delight.*)

Blackout

ACT TWO

SCENE 2

Lights come up almost immediately. DEREK *and* SYLVIA *are seated on sofa,* GEORGE *is semi-seated on front edge of desk, his feet still on the floor, and* PEGGY *is on her knees before him; all four hold two or three pages of hastily scribbled scripts. When the players are reading their parts, the lines will be in quotes; lines not in quotes are their in-character normal lines.*

GEORGE. "You're going to have a child?" (*Giggles.*) "Ridiculous!"

PEGGY. (*Slumps in chagrin and gives pleading look toward* DEREK.) So help me, if he does that *once more,* I'll *scream!*

DEREK. You *are* rather missing the spirit of the moment, George.

SYLVIA. Yes, can't you make the laughter just a teensy bit more *scornful?*

GEORGE. (*Hurt.*) That *was* scornful!

PEGGY. George, *no* one demonstrating *scorn* does it with a *giggle!*

GEORGE. (*Stands.*) Okay! That's it! I give up! Let's all register at the poorhouse and *forget* this stupid scheming.

DEREK. (*Rises, moves toward him.*) Now, now, George, don't take on so. You're not the first person to be miscast in the history of the theater. Scorn's just not your bag. Here— (*Hands him script.*) you take *my* part, and let Sylvia do Peggy's. After all, I'm much more likely to be nasty to Sylvia than you are to Uncle's nurse.

SYLVIA. (*Also rising and moving deskward.*) You can say that again!

PEGGY. (*Getting to her feet.*) But honestly—would a trained nurse be likely to come down with a disease like this? (*Points toward* SYLVIA's *script.*)

SYLVIA. Like what? We never *named* the stupid sickness.

PEGGY. I don't mean like this *disease*—I mean *come down* with it like this! (*Takes script from* SYLVIA.) All this moaning nobility—instead of heading for the penicillin!

GEORGE. Peggy's got a point.

SYLVIA. But her nurse's cap hides it.

DEREK. (*Before the women can come to blows.*) Hold it! Save your squabbling for *after* we're rich!

GEORGE. Derek's right. After all, Peggy can play a sickly patient a lot better than I can play a cad.

DEREK. Exactly. So it's all settled. Everybody switch scripts! (*They do so; the men swap with each other, and so do the women, during:*)

GEORGE. I wish you'd thought of this sooner. I practically have my lines committed to memory.

DEREK. We *all* do, George. Just think of this as a major rewrite in New Haven.

GEORGE. Just before we close out of town! (*Couples are moving to swap locales,* DEREK *and* SYLVIA *toward desk,* GEORGE *and* PEGGY *toward sofa, during:*)

DEREK. Oh, sit down, both of you, and watch some real performers at work! (*They ao, and* SYLVIA *kneels and* DEREK *half-sits on front edge of desk.*) Ready, darling?

SYLVIA. (*Squinting at new script.*) Ready as I'll ever be!

DEREK. Okay, here goes— (*Gets into character, which is an outrageously hammy version of scorn, as* SYLVIA's *will be of misery.*) "You're going to have a child?" (*Scornful laugh.*) "Ridiculous!"

SYLVIA. "It isn't! It isn't!"

DEREK. "Well, don't blame *me* for it!"

SYLVIA. "What? Have you forgotten what you said, when we were trapped in that stalled elevator, and you took me in your arms, and murmurred—"

DEREK. (*Quoting emotionlessly, nodding with boredom.*) " 'You're a girl after my own heart!' "

SYLVIA. "Oh, darling, you remember! Then I don't mind the terrible price I'm forced to pay!"

DEREK. (*Relieved, stands up straight.*) "That's nice to know. Well—see you around. Can I call you a cab?"

SYLVIA. (*Rises wrathfully.*) "Is that all you have to say?! And to think I thought of you as my knight in armor—a regular Sir Galahad!"

DEREK. "Ha! If *I* get on a horse, I get *nauseous* and usually throw up!"

SYLVIA. (*Sighs.*) "I never *was* a good judge of character. I guess I'll kill myself."

DEREK. (*Becoming concerned.*) "No, wait! You mustn't talk like that!"

SYLVIA. (*With new hope.*) "Ah—then you *do* have finer feelings!"

DEREK. "You always did know the way to a man's heart."

SYLVIA. (*Takes his hands.*) "Then, you really *do* love me? You'll *marry* me?"

DEREK. "Just try and stop me!"

SYLVIA. (*Leans her cheek against his chest.*) "How foolish do you think I am?!"

DEREK. "Don't worry. When I tell Oliver what's happened, we can really clean up!" (*It's the end, and* GEORGE *and* PEGGY *start polite applause, but stop as* DEREK *moves away from* SYLVIA *toward them, frowning, and says:*) Are you sure that's enough, George? That last bit about cleaning up—it's the nearest you come to a mention of money. Oliver might miss the hint, after you let him eavesdrop on your little scene.

GEORGE. Don't worry—as soon as we *realize*—quote-unquote—that he *heard* us, we'll spell the money part out for him in no uncertain terms.

DEREK. (*Shrugs, moves back toward* SYLVIA.) Okay, if you're satisfied with it—but I think more explicit terms will do a lot more good. (SYLVIA *will join him in half-sit on desk-front, during:*)

PEGGY. Is that what *your* script does?

SYLVIA. Try it, and see for yourself.

PEGGY. All right. Ready, George?

GEORGE. As soon as you lie back a bit. Remember, you're imitating *Camille*.

PEGGY. But let's leave out the coughing, shall we?

GEORGE. (*Turning to sit on edge of sofa facing her as she lies back weakly, languishingly.*) Anything you say. Ready?

PEGGY. Ready.

GEORGE. (*Takes one of her hands, pats it solicitously, and all his lines will be as anguished as hers are sickly.*) "A fatal disease? It can't be true! It can't, it can't!"

PEGGY. "Darling, don't cry, please! I cannot bear the pain I see in your face!"

GEORGE. "We've got to get you medical help, fast!"

PEGGY. "It's too late for that! The situation is hopeless!"

GEORGE. "There's got to be a way out! There's got to be!"

PEGGY. "Money would help. Lots of money. Lots and lots of it."

GEORGE. (*Off script.*) Really, Derek! Isn't that laying it on a bit thick?

DEREK. You're jealous 'cause I'm a better playwright than you are.

GEORGE. That'll be the day! (*To* PEGGY.) Where were we?

PEGGY. (*Cuing him.*) "Money would help. Lots of money. Lots and lots of it."

GEORGE. (*Scanning page for place.*) Ah, found it! (*Back into character.*) "But where can you get such a great amount?"

PEGGY. "I thought—pernaps—you might saddle Oliver with that debt . . ."

GEORGE. "What? That pinchpenny? That tyrant? That heartless creature?"

PEGGY. "But—couldn't you—do it over *me?*"

GEORGE. "Well—it's certainly worth a try!"

PEGGY. "I'd be no worse off than I am now."

GEORGE. "That's for darn sure!"

PEGGY. "Then—you're going to do it?"

GEORGE. "The moment I see Oliver!"

PEGGY. "Don't do anything you'll regret later—it's so sloppily sentimental of you!"

GEORGE. "Where you're concerned, the sky's the limit!" (DEREK *and* SYLVIA *applaud heartily as* PEGGY *sits up.*)

DEREK. Bravo! Bravo!

SYLVIA. What he really means is "Author! Author!"

GEORGE. (*Stands.*) Well, whatever the merits of the script, I'd better start learning it. Then, when Oliver comes in—

PEGGY. (*Stands.*) Say! . . . What *about* when Oliver comes in? We can't *both* do our little scenes! We'd cramp each other's style. Only two of us should be here first, and the other two after.

SYLVIA. That's logical.

DEREK. The hell it is! Little Miss Hygeine may be fooling you, but not me!

GEORGE. Derek, what *are* you babbling about?

DEREK. The simple fact that if we let you two do your piece first, what's to prevent your both galloping off with all the simoleons?!

PEGGY. And what's to prevent *you* doing the same, if *you* go first?!

SYLVIA. Damn it, *somebody's* got to go first?! Oliver may be back any minute—!

GEORGE. Well—maybe one couple could hide and listen in while the other couple—

DEREK. Hide where? Up on the bookshelf, or in a desk drawer?!

PEGGY. But we've *got* to figure out some way to—

SYLVIA. Wait! I've got it! We switch partners!

DEREK. We what?

PEGGY. Of course! It's perfect!

GEORGE. What is?

SYLVIA. You dope! Derek and *I* have common interests, and you and Peggy do, too! So if I do one scene with you, and Derek does the other one with Peggy—!

DEREK. Aha! We can *each* watch each *other!* A flawless scheme, Sylvia! Where did you ever get such a devious brain?!

SYLVIA. Maybe yours is contagious.

GEORGE. Look, save the fighting for after you're married. Right now, Derek and I have got to memorize new scripts!

PEGGY. Don't *we?*

DEREK. Don't be an idiot! If we *all* learn new scenes, we'd be mixing up the ones we just *did!*

GEORGE. Right. So you girls stay the same, and Derek and I will each learn the other's *original* part, to play opposite the *new* partner, see?

SYLVIA. Okay, great! And Peggy and I will bone up on learning the *old* lines! Come on, Nurse! (*She and* PEGGY *take scripts and exit to garden.*)

GEORGE. (*As he and* DEREK *scowl down at scripts and start pacing.*) I wish there were some way you and I could rehearse each other.

DEREK. Don't be a nerd! It'll be tough enough, learning *new* lines, without listening to *you* reading the *old* ones!

GEORGE. Say—wait! Which lines are we supposed to learn? The ones we just did, or the ones we were *originally* going to do before we switched parts?

DEREK. Why—um—the ones we just did, of course. I think . . .

GEORGE. Well, I hope the *girls* know that! (*He and* DEREK *will now pace, reading and mumbling, for a few moments; then* PEGGY *and* SYLVIA *re-enter, fast.*)

SYLVIA. Hey, listen, we were just getting our lines down pat, when it occurred to us that you might be memorizing the wrong—

DEREK. Relax. It occurred to us, too, but we finally decided—

PEGGY. Hey, everybody! I think I hear *Oliver* coming!

OLIVER. (*Off.*) George? Derek? Where *is* everybody, anyhow?!

DEREK. (*Grabbing every script, all of which he'll put in desk.*) There's not a moment to lose! George—Sylvia—get out of here, quick! (*They start for garden.*) Peggy, get into position, fast! (*As* GEORGE *and* SYLVIA *leave, practically loping,* PEGGY *obediently gets into position* on the sofa, *as* DEREK *slams drawer on scripts, whirls, and takes his stance* half-sitting on desk. *For a moment, they do not see the dread significance of this—then, as BOTH react with horror—*OLIVER *steps into room, and a desperate* DEREK *launches their insane "deception" with:*) "You're going to have a child?" (*Gives scornful laugh, as* OLIVER *reacts and remains standing just inside room, listening.*) "Ridiculous!"

PEGGY. (*Gapes a second, then sickly says her other-scheme line:*) "Darling, don't cry, please! I cannot bear the pain I see in your face!'' (*Now BOTH know they are doomed; but—like boaters who keep rowing back from an approaching tidal wave ten times their speed—they struggle valiantly onward:*)

DEREK. ''Well, don't blame *me* for it!''

PEGGY. ''It's too late for that! The situation is hopeless!''

DEREK. '' 'You're a girl after my own heart!' '' (*By now, their readings become mechanical, automatic, as their despair grows into total defeatism.*)

PEGGY. ''Money would help. Lots of money. Lots and lots of it.''

DEREK. ''That's nice to know. Well—see you around. Can I call you a cab?''

PEGGY. ''I thought—perhaps—you might saddle Oliver with that debt . . .''

DEREK. ''Ha! If I get on a horse, I get nauseous and usually throw up!''

PEGGY. ''But—couldn't you—do it over *me?*'' (*The image is too much; she starts to stifle a giggle.*)

DEREK. (*Fighting laughter himself, but dogged to the end.*) ''No, wait! You mustn't talk like that!''

PEGGY. ''I'd be no worse off than I am now.'' (*Covers her face, but quakes with suppressed laughter.*)

DEREK. (*So near laughter, now, he turns his back on room, facing desk, leaning his fisted knuckles on it and trying not to choke with mirth as he plows onward:*) ''You always did know the way to a man's heart.''

PEGGY. (*Sits up, but valiantly continues, quaking.*) ''Then—you're going to do it?''

DEREK. (*Guffaws, then manages to say:*) ''Just try and stop me!''

PEGGY. (*Laughs aloud, then chokes out:*) ''Don't do anything you'll regret later—it's so— (*Half-speaks, half-giggles rest of line:*) —sloppily sentimental of you!''

DEREK. (*Turns toward her, finally, holds out his arms helplessly, and finishes:*) ''Don't worry. When I tell Oliver what's happened, we can really *clean up!''* (*Howls with laughter, lurches to sofa, sits beside* PEGGY, *and both of them just rock back and laugh wildly, as a bewildered* OLIVER *stares at them in total confusion. As they start getting their breaths,* GEORGE *and* SYLVIA *peek in from garden, curiously.*)

GEORGE. We—uh—we heard laughter . . .

SYLVIA. (*As both move tentatively into room.*) Has—um—anything *nice* happened to somebody, maybe—?

DEREK. (*Exchanges a glance with* PEGGY, *speaks conspiratorily.*) Should we do it?

PEGGY. (*Shrugs.*) No point in suffering alone!

DEREK. (*Stands.*) That was the hysteria of *loss* you heard, my friends. Perhaps, uh, *your* luck might be better—when—you— (*Pointedly cuing them.*) —*continue what you two were discussing in the garden*—?! (*Starts toward* OLIVER, *and* PEGGY *hastily rises and moves to join him, during:*)

PEGGY. We'll just stand over here and give you moral support . . .

DEREK. On your marks—get set— (GEORGE *scurries to sit on front edge of sofa, and looks bewildered as* SYLVIA *rushes to drop to her knees before desk, but it's too late, as:*)

PEGGY. *Take it!*

GEORGE. (*Confused but game, speaks toward* SYLVIA'S *back.*) ''A fatal disease? It can't be true! It can't, it can't!''

SYLVIA. (*Who during his speech has pivoted on her knees to face him, says in bewilderment:*) ''It isn't! It isn't!''

[*NOTE: The motivation for* GEORGE *and* SYLVIA *to go on, unlike the motive (helpless amusement) of* DEREK *and* PEGGY, *is simple bewilderment: They know it sounds all wrong, yet, after all,* OLIVER *is listening, and* DEREK *and* PEGGY—*whenever* SYLVIA *or* GEORGE *may cast them a look of confusion—are just wicked enough to frown and do* sub rosa *gestures toward*

OLIVER, *signifying that a continuation of the scripted words is somehow vital. And so, dazed but game,* GEORGE *and* SYLVIA *manage to go on to the idiotic end, without really understanding* why *they are doing so.*]

GEORGE. (*As if he meant* mental *help, considering her last line.*) "We've got to get you medical help, fast!"

SYLVIA. (*Gets uncertainly to her feet, during:*) "What? Have you forgotten what you said, when we were trapped in that stalled elevator, and you took me in your arms, and murmurred—"

GEORGE. (*Stands, continuing script as if continuing her line:*) "There's got to be a way out! There's got to be!"

SYLVIA. "Oh, darling, you remember! Then I don't mind the terrible price I'm forced to pay!" (*More because it feels safer than standing alone than for any rational reason,* GEORGE *moves to her, during:*)

GEORGE. "But where can you get such a great amount?"

SYLVIA. (*Similarly moving toward him.*) "Is that all you have to say?! And to think I thought of you as my knight in armor—a regular Sir Galahad!"

GEORGE. (*Takes her hands, now.*) "What? That pinchpenny? That tyrant? That heartless creature?"

OLIVER. (*Looking baffledly from* PEGGY *to* DEREK.) Sir Galahad?

PEGGY/DEREK. *Ssh!* (*Trio faces helpless duo again, for remainder of:*)

SYLVIA. (*Doggedly, at sea.*) "I never *was* a good judge of character. I guess I'll kill myself."

GEORGE. (*Similarly.*) "Well—it's certainly worth a try!"

SYLVIA. (*Although it's insane on the heels of what he said.*) "Ah—then you *do* have finer feelings!"

GEORGE. "That's for darn sure!"

SYLVIA. "Then you really *do* love me? You'll marry me?"

GEORGE. "The moment I see Oliver!"

SYLVIA. (*As per rehearsal, leans her cheek against his chest.*) ''How foolish do you think I am?!''

GEORGE. (*Knowing it's madness, but determined to finish.*) ''Where you're concerned, the sky's the limit!''

(*Then BOTH sag into an embrace of mutual confusion, shaking their heads as if to clear them, while DEREK and PEGGY, no longer needing to look solemn, begin to howl and double up with laughter, as OLIVER looks at them as if they'd gone mad, and—unable to explain, of course—they abruptly flee to front hall, and GEORGE and SYLVIA, breaking their clinch and eager for some sort of explanation, start off after them, during:*)

OLIVER. George—Sylvia—! What in the world is going on here?! Did I just hear *you* propose *marriage* to *Derek's* sweetheart, or what?

GEORGE. Damned if *I* know, Dad!

SYLVIA. It's been a *very* confusing evening!

(*Each has exited on line, and OLIVER is alone; he stands there, blinking, placing fingers to temples, shaking head, trying to recall anything sensible he might have heard, as J.D. enters from hall, looking back curiously over her shoulder until she gets to OLIVER. Then:*)

J.D. Did I miss something? Miss Brent and your nephew are sitting on the staircase laughing like maniacs, and that Sylvia woman and your son are staggering toward them like they've just been mugged! What happened?

OLIVER. I'm not sure—I think Peggy is going to have a baby named Sir Galahad, if Derek doesn't throw up, and George is going to marry Sylvia to give her disease a name. Or something.

J.D. That doesn't make sense.

OLIVER. You're telling me! You're telling me! I need

fresh air. (*Still holding and shaking head, exits to garden; as* J.D. *stares after him,* SANDERS *enters from hall.*)

SANDERS. Excuse me, ma'am, but—that temperance person is here.

J.D. What? Oh, oh, yes, I remember. Well—show her in. Then go and get Miss Brent—I believe Oliver has *her* in mind for salvation—if she can ever stop laughing.

SANDERS. (*Bows slightly.*) Very good, ma'am.

J.D. (*Still slightly fogged by events.*) Mm? *What's* very good?

SANDERS. (*Shrugs.*) Search me. That's butler-talk. (*Turns and exits to hall.*)

(J.D., *still bewildered, turns and moves toward desk, and so does not see* CORA VAN BECK *enter, like an arrow from a bow. She is entirely in black, including her stockings, but wears a scarlet feather boa, and a large red rose that juts from her black straw hat's brim like the prow of a ship; she also carries a large bumbershoot-style umbrella, the ferrule pointed before her like a knight's lance, and she charges across room till she is just behind* J.D.—*who has not seen her yet— and prods her in the rear with the ferrule just as she speaks, both the contact and the voice-level causing* J.D. *to nearly leap through the ceiling:*)

CORA. (*At lung-top.*) DRINKING IS A CURSE! (J.D. *whirls, leaning back in terror against lip of desk, watching as the ferrule manaces her throat.*) Give it up! The Women's League for Dry Distilleries has sent me to save you, yes, you, from the curse of alcohol! Our slogan is, "A foot inside a tavern is a foot inside the grave!" Resist! Fight! You are not alone! Destroy this craving that racks your body, twists your soul, puts pimples on your mind! Feel clean again, all over! Ask now, for the help you direly need! You must want help, or I can give none! So ask for it! Ask for help! Ask! *Ask! ASK!* . . .

J.D. (*Totally terrified.*) *HELLLLLLLLLLLLP—!* (*And as she sustains this anguished cry—.*)

The Curtain Falls

ACT THREE

It is about five minutes later. J.D. *is leading* CORA *from desk area toward hall as curtain rises.*

J.D. Now are you sure you have matters straight, Miss Van Beck?

CORA. I think so, Ms. Culver—the one I want is a Miss Peggy Brent?

J.D. Right.

CORA. (*Near door to hall, now, pauses.*) How far gone is she?

J.D. I fear I am no judge in these matters.

CORA. (*Moves umbrella menacingly.*) You're covering for her!

J.D. Now, *really*, Miss Van Beck—!

CORA. Oh, please call me "Cora."

J.D. Uh—yes, to be sure.

CORA. To be sure of what?

J.D. (*Shrugs.*) Search me. That's lawyer-talk. (*Gestures hallward.*) Now, really, you'd better start looking for Miss Brent. She can't have gotten far.

CORA. But how will I know when I've found her?

J.D. (*Impatient.*) You might try smelling her breath!

(CORA *gives her a look, but exits;* J.D., *much relieved, starts back toward desk.* WU *enters behind her, from hall.*)

WU. *Psssst!* (J.D. *jumps, turns about.*)

J.D. Don't *do* that, Charlie! If one more person sneaks up on me tonight—!

WU. (*Approaches her anxiously, interrupting:*) I'm getting nervous, Jenny. This Oliver Stratton *can't* be as stupid as he acts—!

J.D. That's all you know. Oliver is a *career* idiot!

WU. But this hanging around wasn't part of our plan. I'm getting antsy. Why don't I just bump him off and scram, huh?

J.D. (*Hastily clamps hand over* WU's *mouth.*) Quiet, you numbskull! Someone might overhear you!

WU. (*Grunts and struggles free of hand.*) Okay-okay! . . . But— (*Lowers voice.*) why can't I just let him have it, right here, and get it over with?

J.D. You don't *know?* Honestly, Charlie—how many men have you murdered in your lifetime?

WU. Oh . . . let me see—there was—no, wait, that didn't quite come off—but—

J.D. (*Intensely, but not loudly.*) How many?!

WU. (*Embarrassed.*) None, really.

J.D. *What?*

WU. (*Defensively.*) I tried—honest I did—and I *scared* a *lot* of them—and *one* time, believe it or not, I *almost*—

J.D. As I have always suspected, you are somewhat inept in the fine art of life-taking, Charlie. You see . . . (*Seats* WU *beside her on sofa, speaks with quiet patience, as a teacher to a somewhat likeable but dopey child.*) When it becomes necessary to rid one's heart of a painful knot, a knot put there by another person—in this case, Oliver Stratton—and the person one has hired—that's you, Charlie—is supposed to resort to permanent knot-releasing —sometimes called "murder"—and seems to have forgotten one essential in this fine art, one feels obliged to point that oversight out to him, do you see?

WU. (*Who has been listening with smiling patience, takes a breath, and starts a nod he does not complete, on:*) . . . No. (*Beat.*) What essential have I forgotten?

J.D. (*A shout.*) You're not supposed to get *caught!* (*Instant reverse-business as* WU *clamps hand on* J.D.'s *mouth, and as* J.D. *struggles and grunts:*)

WU. Quiet, you numbskull! (*Gets glare, realizes, releases her, cringes.*) Sorry, boss.

J.D. (*Adjusting rumpled clothing and composure.*) Why I ever hooked up with you, I'll never know! That day you came into my office, trying to "latch onto a sharp mouthpiece to keep you outa stir," I had to go and get my glorious-vengeance notion!

WU. (*Wistfully.*) I *try* hard, Jenny . . .

J.D. And that's another thing! Since when did we get on a first-name basis?

WU. The first time you called me "Charlie."

J.D. That's different!

WU. Why? It's *my* first name.

J.D. (*Almost retorts, gives it up.*) Okay. You win. Now let's get back to the problem: I'll spell it out in alphabet blocks. The secret of success in the murder game is *not to get caught,* right?

WU. That sounds logical.

J.D. But if you come to this house, and then Oliver is killed, and then you go away, the police will certainly *think unkindly* of your action! They will probably suspect you within *thirty-seven seconds!* And then they will go *looking* for you, Dumdum!

WU. But they'll be looking in *Tibet,* and I won't *be* in Tibet.

J.D. That's exactly my point! If you are not there, they will say, "Then whence *was* this lama?!", and somebody is sure to remember that *I* was the liaison between you and Oliver, and then they will start questioning *me* about you! And do you know what I will *do,* in that event—?

WU. You wouldn't *tattle?*

J.D. Let me put it this way: If I get sent to the electric chair, I'm not going to take it sitting down! (*Realizes how dumb this sounds as* WU *reacts, and clarifies:*) What I mean is—if I go, you go!

WU. (*With a sullen pout.*) Snitcher.

J.D. You *bet* I am! . . . *However—!* (WU *perks up hopefully.*) If you will just follow *my* plan, Charlie, no guilt will descend upon *either* of us.

Wu. Why not?

J.D. (*Patiently.*) Because if he goes *off* with you tonight and is never seen again, no one will think anything of it, because no one *expects* to ever see him again, see?!

Wu. Ah! But if I bump him off here in the house—

J.D. We . . . are . . . both . . . *doomed!* Now do you follow? Just do it the way we planned, and— Say, are you *sure* he won't float?

Wu. Wearing a cement-filled inner-tube, with an anchor tied to each leg, and a bowling ball glued to his thumb?

J.D. Don't overdo it—he'll be too heavy to push off the pier! (*Stands.*) Come on, now, Charlie. I'll tell Oliver that a ticket-agent friend of mine has managed to get him last-minute passage if we hurry down to the pier right away! No, wait—if we both go, it might look too anxious. You go round him up and bring him in here, to me.

Wu. (*Starts toward hall, then stops.*) It seems kind of a shame. I hate to bump a guy off for no reason.

J.D. I am *paying* you to do it!

Wu. (*Brightens.*) I *knew* there was a reason!

(*Exits; J.D. stands looking after him, nervously tapping the knuckles of one fist into the opposing palm, as OLIVER—back from his quest for fresh air—strolls in from garden behind her, sees her, strolls up behind her, and—*)

OLIVER. *Ah* there, J.D.! (*She screams, leaps off the floor, turning in mid-air and coming down facing him, terrified.*) Did I startle you?

J.D. (*Recovering hastily.*) Of course not. But—what are you doing here? Why aren't you up in your room packing?

OLIVER. I was just getting some air to clear my head, and—well, it did the trick. I'm thinking quite clearly now, and—I don't think I'll become a monk after all.

J.D. But you've *got* to! . . . That is—uh—*not* become a monk? Whyever not?

OLIVER. I've just remembered that ships make me sea-sick. Besides which, standing on deck would remind me of my lost love, and I might get so despondent I'd jump overboard!

J.D. (*Brightens, claps a hand on his shoulder.*) And who could blame you!

OLIVER. You're a good friend, J.D. But—no, I'd best stay here. Besides, I can hardly leave with my will in such a shambles, can I? I *was* leaving things to Peggy, but then I got to thinking about George, and of course Derek's not so bad when you get used to him, and I recently discovered that Sylvia has her good points as well, and—

J.D. Look! Take the boat! You can think it all out while you're en route, and wire me any changes in the will, and—when you get to port near Tibet—if you still feel the same way, you can always come back—and you'll have had a nice vacation in the meantime!

OLIVER. (*Hesitates, toys with the notion, then shakes his head.*) Mmmm—no. No, I hate to leave things up in the air. After all, I could die before I even *reached* the boat! (J.D. *covers her guilt with a wide and unconvincing smile.*) And with Sylvia's knight in armor getting nauseous, and Peggy's illegitimate child coming down with a fatal disease—or was it the other way around—?

J.D. (*Totally at sea.*) How the hell should *I* know?!

OLIVER. Ah well. No matter, no matter. I can set things aright in just a few simple words . . . J.D.—take a will! (J.D. *almost speaks, then sighs, goes obediently to desk, sits, gets paper and pen, and poises pen to write.*)

J.D. Ready when you are, Oliver.

OLIVER. (*Takes a stance before sofa, ponders; then:*) I, Oliver Stratton, being of sound mind—

J.D. (*Unable to suppress it, mutters audibly:*) Ha!

OLIVER. I beg your pardon—?

J.D. It's nothing.

OLIVER. (*Shrugs, resumes.*) . . . of sound mind, hereby bequeath all of my worldly—um—oh, *you* write it

up, J.D., you know the legal gobbledegook better than anybody. What *is* the terminology for everything I own, the
house, the land, the cash, and suchlike?

J.D. "The whole kit and kaboodle."

OLIVER. Really?

J.D. (*Scribbling.*) Only we say it in Latin.

OLIVER. What did lawyers use in Ancient Rome?

J.D. (*Still scribbling.*) Greek.

OLIVER. Why don't they ever use the language of their
own country?

J.D. Then who'd need a lawyer? (*As* OLIVER *nods at the
wisdom of this, she finishes.*) There! All written except for
the important part: Who is the legatee?

OLIVER. The what?

J.D. The lucky winner.

OLIVER. Oh. Well, um—hmm, this is the part I hate. Ah,
wait! Tell you what: Leave that part blank, why don't you,
and we can fill in the name as soon as I make a decision.
Could *you* suggest a name?

J.D. "J.D. Culver" has a nice ring to it . . .

OLIVER. But—that's you!

J.D. I'd give the money a good home, Oliver.

OLIVER. Don't tease, J.D.

J.D. Who's teasing!

OLIVER. But—you're a successful lawyer!

J.D. Couldn't I be a successful *rich* lawyer?

OLIVER. I couldn't do that to you, my dear. After all, we
are friends. You don't *know* the anguish of being loaded
with dough.

J.D. I could *learn* . . .

OLIVER. Ah, but, if you knew the responsibilities, the
annoyances, the terrible taxes, the onus of living in
luxury—?

J.D. I'd bear up somehow—!

OLIVER. Enough! Just leave that thing as it is, for now—
(*Will move deskward as he speaks.*) And we'll go round up

the others, get them in here, and after I tell them my decision about Tibetan monkhood, I'll figure out whose name goes into the winner's slot. (*Is leaning over* J.D.'s *shoulder, now.*) Where do I sign?

J.D. (*Indicating.*) Right here, but— (*Pauses as* OLIVER *takes pen, signs the paper, and then returns pen to her.*) Oliver, you really ought to reconsider this Tibet thing. After all the *plans* I've made—that is—*you've* made, and—!

OLIVER. Ah, that reminds me! Has that temperance person shown up yet?

J.D. In spades! (*As* OLIVER *reacts, continues:*) She's out looking for Miss Brent, somewhere in the house—

OLIVER. (*Takes* J.D.'s *arm, tows her hallward.*) Admirable! Let us find her. Who knows—should she be a person of sterling character—I might very well leave all the money to *her!*

(*They exit to hall, and immediately* GEORGE, SYLVIA, DEREK *and* PEGGY *enter from garden, and move toward liquor.*)

DEREK. I thought they'd *never* leave! I'm perishing from thirst! (*Will pour himself a stiff, iceless drink; none of his conspirators will use ice, either.*)

PEGGY. I still don't see why we couldn't come in while they were here. (*Finds different bottle, pours drink of her own, strolls hallward with it.*)

DEREK. Because Oliver might start asking what the four of us were up to, a moment ago, and I don't have any satisfactory answers! Do *you?!* (*Since his question is rhetorical, she simply sighs and sips her drink without responding, during:*)

GEORGE. (*Staring hallward as* SYLVIA *pours her own drink.*) He must think we've all gone bananas! I wonder what he made of what we were saying?

SYLVIA. What *he* made!? George, dear, *I* can't even

figure out what the two of *us* were talking about! . . . Drink?

GEORGE. Why not! Whatever it is, make it a double. (*As* SYLVIA *pours him a stiff one,* PEGGY—*after a peek out into the hall—moves back toward group, on:*)

PEGGY. There's the oddest-looking little old lady out in the front hall.

DEREK. Probably collecting for some charity. Sanders will take care of it—that's one of his duties.

SYLVIA. How can he *afford* it?! (*Hands drink to* GEORGE.)

GEORGE. Thanks. I really need this. (*Drains it in one gulp, hands empty to her.*) Better make this one a triple.

SYLVIA. (*Tosses off her own drink, takes his glass.*) How did *I* get elected bartender? (*But she is obediently pouring a really stiff one as* CORA VAN BECK *enters from hall, sees her, and reacts.*) It'd be simpler to just drink right from the bottle! (*As she lifts filled glass, but before she can extend it toward* GEORGE, *she is prevented by* CORA *grabbing her arm.*) Hey!

CORA. Drop it! Drop it, Miss Brent!

SYLVIA. "Miss Brent"?! You watch your language! (*Struggles to get free.*) And let go of my arm, you old bat!

CORA. Never! You need help! And I'm here to give it!

SYLVIA. (*Still struggling as* OTHERS *watch in fascination.*) You're the one who needs *help,* sister, and you're *about* to get it! (*Balls up fist of free hand, ready to deck her.*)

CORA. (*Releases her, takes a back-step.*) But you can't give up without a fight! Fight it! Fight the craving!

SYLVIA. (*Hands drink to* GEORGE *without looking his way, the better to get her hands free so that she can jam her fists against her hips and glare at* CORA, *during:*) Listen, kiddo, the only craving of which I am conscious is a craving to pull that feather boa taut across your windpipe!

CORA. But my dear, I'm here to *save* you! (*Starts searching her own person.*) Here, If you'll only just read this—?

That's odd. What in the world did I do with—? Oh, of course! (*Brightens and starts for desk, the trio of drink-holders sipping slowly as they watch her in curious attention.*) I left them on the desk when I was speaking with that lawyer lady—! If you'll just study the findings of my organization—

SYLVIA. Listen, honey, you're twisting the wrong wrist. The butler is the man who takes care of peddlers.

CORA. (*At desk, rummaging through small stack of pamphlets.*) But my dear, I'm not selling anything—I'm here to save you from the curse of alcohol, Miss Brent!

GEORGE. (*Catches on.*) Oh! You're the hoozy about the whatsis! That Oliver sent for.

CORA. (*Drops pamphlets, whirls on him.*) Who're you calling a floozy?!

DEREK. (*While* SYLVIA, *now unimpeded, refills her own glass.*) Not "floozy"! The gentleman said "hoozy"! You know—the whatchamacallit lady!

PEGGY. (*To* CORA.) The title they can't seem to think of is "temperance representative."

GEORGE. But that's all a mistake.

SYLVIA. There was a misunderstanding during dinner.

DEREK. So we don't require your services after all. (*Then* ALL FOUR *simultaneously drain their drinks.*)

CORA. (*Reacts.*) But you're practically *bathing* in the stuff!

PEGGY. Look, if you *must* save somebody, there's a *real* little lush on the premises who had too much Hudson tonight.

SYLVIA. Yes, why don't you go work on Wu?

CORA. How dare you!

GEORGE. It's the gentleman's *name*, dear lady. He is a monk, from Tibet.

CORA. Don't you mean a panda?

DEREK. We don't mean a furry little animal, we mean a lama.

CORA. (*Still at sea.*) But—?

SYLVIA. (*Before the error can continue farther.*) The kind with *one* "l"! You know—the cowl-and-scowl set.

CORA. Oh. But Tibet is out of my territory.

SYLVIA. Well, so am *I!* (*Indicates* PEGGY.) *This* is Miss Brent!

PEGGY. (*Raises empty glass to* CORA.) Cheers.

CORA. (*Moves to her.*) Fear not, you poor darling. I am here to give you the secret of everlasting happiness!

GEORGE. I hope you mean the combination to the safe?

CORA. What safe?

DEREK. There goes *that* hope!

PEGGY. But I'm truly sorry to tell you there's been a mistake. *I* mostly use alcohol as a *disinfectant.*

CORA. Then—why *was* I sent for?

PEGGY. You'll have to ask Mister Stratton.

GEORGE. Yes, he's the one decided to have you come here.

DEREK. Let him wriggle out of it by himself.

SYLVIA. (*Picking up bottle.*) Come on, gang, let's have our drinks out in the garden. (*Starts that way, the trio of empty-glassed drinkers moving after her.*) As soon as Oliver sails, the rest of my life bodes to be spent shuttling between the Bronx and the Automat. (*Exits on:*) I need one more look at that Long Island moon. (OTHERS *wave cheerily at* CORA *and follow* SYLVIA *off.*)

CORA. (*Baffled, turns and starts frowningly sorting through her pamphlets on the desktop.*) There must be *something* here to cover this situation . . . let's see . . . (*Reading aloud, musingly.*) "You Cannot Be High *and* Dry" . . . "Don't Take Your Car to Get Oiled" . . . "Look Out for Your Liver" . . . Ah! The very one!—"Partying Is Such Sweet Sorrow"! (*Grabs it up, heads gardenward.*) Maybe I can *read* some sense into them!

(CORA *has barely exited to garden when* SANDERS *and*

JANE, *moving furtively, enter from hall and scurry toward safe.*)

JANE. (*Anxiously.*) Herbert, are you sure it's safe—?

SANDERS. (*Removes stick of TNT from inside his jacket as she raises picture to expose safe to view.*) Safe for us, but unsafe for the safe! (*Takes roll of tape from pocket, starts attaching TNT to front of steel door, its fuse dangling.*) We'll be 'way off in the kitchen when this goes off, and then we can hurry back in here and scoop up the money! . . . Have you got a match?

JANE. I think so . . . (*He keeps taping as she fumbles in her pockets.*) But—what if somebody is standing near it when it explodes? Or what if it explodes before you and I get clear of the room?

SANDERS. Will you stop worrying?! (*Stick is secured to safe; he repockets tape and will turn and speak to* JANE *as she continues search.*) In answer to your first question, there is nobody here, so nobody will get hurt. As to your second question, this is a slow-burning fuse. It will be at least ten minutes before it reaches the TNT, plenty of time for us to get to the kitchen, I'm sure.

JANE. (*Finds wooden match, hands it to him.*) How sure? This stuff is dangerous!

SANDERS. (*Ignites fuse.*) Every successful venture involves a bit of risk, Jane. There!

JANE. Oh, dear! (*Turns Downstage, cringes, covers face with hands.*) I can't look!

SANDERS. You won't have to! (*Lowers picture to hide safe and burning fuse.*)

JANE. I don't want to listen, either!

(*Uncovers face, but has eyes scrunched shut, crouches and holds heels of hands to her ears.* SANDERS *has hastened toward door, realizes he is alone, turns and sees her, rushes back and starts to tug her arm.*)

SANDERS. Come *on*, Jane, come *on!*

JANE. (*Maintains crouch, but uncovers ears and squints at him.*) Did you say something?

SANDERS. Jane, we've got to get *out* of here! Why are you *standing* there?!

JANE. (*Realizes, horrified.*) I can't move! I'm paralyzed with fear! Help me, Herbert, help me!

SANDERS. (*Exasperated.*) Good grief, all right!

(*Sweeps her manfully up into his arms and carries her out into hall; in about two seconds, he comes backing into room again, still carrying her, followed by a curious* OLIVER *and* J.D.)

OLIVER. Sanders, what in the world are you two doing?

SANDERS. Uh . . . *Fire drill!* That's it! We *always* have them, sir, just in case. One can't be too careful.

J.D. Very praiseworthy, I'm sure, but would you stop it for now, please? (*Starts toward desk.*) We need you two for a technicality.

OLIVER. Yes, put her down and come over here, Sanders. It seems I signed my will without having the requisite two witnesses.

SANDERS. (*Reluctantly sets a frozen* JANE *on her feet.*) Do we have to *read* it first?

J.D. No, that won't be necessary.

SANDERS. Good! Come *on*, Jane! (*Takes her arm and half-drags her to desk, fast.*) Where do we sign?

J.D. Let me see—where did that thing go, anyhow? It must be mixed up in all that temperance woman's papers—ah, here it is!

JANE. Sign it, Herbert, sign it!

OLIVER. Jane, you seem upset. Is there anything wrong? It's only a last will and testament . . . ?

JANE. (*Glances safeward.*) I wish you'd change the subject!

J.D. (*Smooths will out on desk, extends pen.*) Here, Sanders, you sign first. Oliver *has* signed it already, which is a bit unorthodox, but if you'll just take his word for it that this *is his* signature, then I'm sure your after-the-fact witnessing will be quite legal, and—

SANDERS. (*Grabs pen from her hand, glares.*) Will you shut up and get out of my way?! (*Frantically starts scribbling name on paper.*)

OLIVER. Really, Sanders, there is no call for that sort of explosion! (*JANE immediately reacts with a loud wail.*) Why, Jane—what's come over you?

JANE. *Nothing*, you old fool, and I'd like to *keep* it that way! (*Stresses this with a fearful safeward glance, as she grabs pen from SANDERS and starts signing will.*)

J.D. There, now it's all legal. You and Sanders may leave, now, or continue your fire drill.

SANDERS. Oh, thank you, thank you! (*He and JANE gallop doorward, but conscience makes them pause just short of exit.*) Un—Mister Stratton, sir—

JANE. You don't intend to *stay* in here, do you?

OLIVER. Why—just for a short drink—then I've really got to fly!

JANE. *I'll* say you do! And higher than you think!

OLIVER. I beg your pardon?

SANDERS. Some other time. Come on, Jane! (*Sweeps her up into his arms as before, exits on:*) Fire! Fire! Fiiiiiire!

J.D. (*Sniffs air.*) You know—it may be merely the power of suggestion, but—I almost think I *do* smell something burning . . .

OLIVER. (*Sniffs.*) Hmm. So do I! I wonder if anyone ever turned the oven off? We'd better have a look. (*Starts hallward.*)

J.D. Yes, one can't be too careful . . . (*She exits after OLIVER.*)

(*A moment later, a very disgruntled* CORA *enters from*

*garden; she holds the two raggedly torn halves of her
pamphlet, one in each hand; her hat has been pulled
down so that it is now in tatter about her neck, and the
feather boa has been used on her mouth as a gag; she
turns and tosses the ruined pamphlet onto the rear top
of the desk, and is busily disengaging the gag and
removing her wrecked hat, her back toward the hall,
as* WU *enters from there, carrying a .45 automatic; he
sees her, reacts, and hides the gun in his robe, on:*)

WU. Oops! Hi there!

CORA. (*Whirls, sees him.*) Oh. You must be the lush from
Lhasa. Well— (*With a glare gardenward.*) First things first.
They're a tough bunch, but a challenge only makes me
more determined than ever! (*Rolls up sleeves, during.*) I'm
going to improve their lives if I have to kill them! (*Grabs up
a fresh pamphlet from desk, brandishes it.*) Onward! Onward to health and happiness! (*Gallops out into the garden.*)

WU. Jeepers, what a household! (*Hastens to liquor,
pours drink.*) The sooner I clear out of here, the better! (*As
he tosses off drink,* OLIVER *and* J.D. *re-enter.*)

OLIVER. Strange—the burning odor seems strongest in
here . . .

J.D. Yes, but what could it—? Oh! Wu Chang!

WU. (*Instantly assuming character, bows.*) This humble
one has decided it is time to depart.

OLIVER. You mean right now? But—I haven't had a
chance to say goodbye to anybody.

WU. You must put aside your worldly ties, Oliver Stratton, if you are to be worthy of acceptance by my monastic
associates. We go, now or never.

OLIVER. I understand that, Wu, but I've been having
second thoughts, and—

J.D. (*Urging him hallward.*) On the boat, Oliver, on the
boat, *remember?* The cruise will give you time to really
think things out.

OLIVER. Oh, drat. Well—I guess you're right, J.D. Will you make my farewells for me?

J.D. Certainly. And bon voyage to both of you! (OLIVER *turns and exits;* WU *winks conspiratorially at* J.D., *takes out gun to show her, repockets it, then squares shoulders and exits after* OLIVER; J.D. *instantly does a little dance of glee.*) Revenge! Revenge at last! Ah-ha-ha-ha—! Whoops! (*Stops and smooths her dress in decorum as quartet of drinkers enter from garden with emptied glasses and emptied bottle; they proceed back to liquor and start making refills, during:*)

DEREK. Boy, that is the most *persistent* dame!

SYLVIA. Think she'll get out of that tree all right?

PEGGY. Probably. It took both the men to put her up there.

GEORGE. And I'm not up to doing it again! (*To* J.D.) Have you seen Dad? He's the only one who can call her off!

J.D. I daresay you're right, since he's the one who sent for her. However, I am sorry to say that your father has already departed. (*All four react with varying degrees of dismay.*)

PEGGY. Just like that?

SYLVIA. Without picking an heir.

DEREK. Or leaving the combination?

GEORGE. Or saying goodbye?

J.D. There was no time. He asked me to make his apologies. (*Despondently, all four set down their glasses on table.*)

DEREK. When I think of all we've gone through, tonight!

PEGGY. And for nothing!

SYLVIA. I could cry!

GEORGE. I could join you! (*To* J.D.) I suppose it's all right now for you to tell us who finally hit the jackpot—?

J.D. (*Realizes.*) Holy jumping catfish! *Nobody!*

DEREK. You mean the money just stays in the safe?

J.D. No, no, I mean he signed the will and had it witnessed, but he never told me whose name went into the beneficiary-space. Why, *anyone* could put his or her name into the blank area and inherit the entire Stratton fortune!

SYLVIA. (*Very casual, since significance of this has not yet dawned on J.D., who keeps casting anxious glances hallward, her thoughts on revenge.*) Uh . . . just—um—where *is* this piece of paper?

J.D. Mm? Oh, over on the desk. Why?

SYLVIA. Ohhhh—no *special* reason. . . .

(*There is one beat here, while all remain in place, and then the foursome bolt madly toward the desk en masse, but DEREK gets there first, grabs up pen and paper, and with a shrieking trio in pursuit, runs madly around the room, scribbling as he moves, ending up with a leap onto the desk, and a triumphant wave of the paper aloft, on:*)

DEREK. Too late! It's done! It's mine, all mine! (*Pursuers slump and sigh unhappily, giving up.*) This is the proudest moment of my life!

SYLVIA. (*Ecstatic.*) And mine, too, darling! (*He just looks at her; she sombers slightly.*) Old pal . . . ? (*No response; she slumps, tries wistfully:*) Kindly stranger—? (*With more steel in her spine and rasp in her voice:*) No-good, lowdown, rotten, repulsive—!

GEORGE. (*Interrupts before she can get to the noun.*) It won't work, Derek! I'll contest the will! *Won't* we, Peggy!

PEGGY. You bet we will!

SYLVIA. (*Brightening.*) On what grounds . . . ?

(*All look toward J.D., DEREK apprehensively, others hopefully, then shift to respective elation and gloom as J.D. shakes her head.*)

J.D. I'm afraid the will is airtight. Once Derek signed

that paper, he gained custody of the entire Stratton fortune. The only man in the world who could negate that will is Oliver, and he's a goner—I mean—he's gone.

GEORGE. (*Grudgingly.*) Well, Derek, now you have everything you've ever desired. And to think it was as simple as signing your name.

SYLVIA. For Derek that's not so simple.

DEREK. Don't be snide, Sylvia. I got this fair and square.

PEGGY. But what about our bargain? All for one, and one for all? You gave your word!

SYLVIA. Yes, but Derek Stratton never kept a promise in his life! *Did* you, Derek!

DEREK. (*Coming down carefully from desktop.*) In money matters, no. But—gazing down upon your plaintive face, I've decided that a *two*-way split isn't such a bad thing, Sylvia. (*As she smiles with radiant relief, he embraces her.*) Wilt thou become my blushing bride?

SYLVIA. *Wilt* I! Wowee, yes! No more Automats—no more train rides to the Bronx—no more sneaking through the Stratton shrubbery—! (*Looks up as* CORA *staggers in, liberally bedizened with oddments of leaf and twig.*)

CORA. You're crazy! All of you people are crazy! I can help just plain drunks, but I can't do a damn thing about certifiable lunatics!

DEREK. Nothing crazy about *me*, dear lady! I have just done the sanest thing I ever did in my life! One flourish of the pen, and I am a permanent resident of seventh heaven! And the only man in the world who could prevent it is Oliver Stratton, and he shall nevermore return! (OLIVER *enters from hall, followed closely by* WU.)

OLIVER. I forgot my toothbrush. (DEREK *gives agonized cry, starts to sob on* SYLVIA'S *shoulder, as she pats his head in sympathy.*) . . . Why—whatever is the matter with Derek?

GEORGE. He just got to seventh heaven and you revoked his visa.

OLIVER. I what?

PEGGY. In simpler terms—you forgot to designate a beneficiary in your will, so Derek signed his name into it and was about to make off with all the money.

OLIVER. Monstrous! Well, I shall soon put *that* aright! Hand over my will at once, young man!

WU. (*Dangerously impatient.*) Hold, Oliver Stratton! If you must persist in this attitude of worldliness, the monkish life is not for you! Either get that toothbrush and come with me now, or I reject your application!

OLIVER. Drat! Ah well, in that case—so long, kids. Can't keep the spiritual life waiting— (*Half-turns, then espies* CORA *in all her dishevelment.*) What the hell is *that?*

CORA. (*With a sniff of disdain.*) I am Cora Van Beck, from the Women's League for Dry Distilleries, come here at *your* request to save a pickled soul from doom!

OLIVER. How did you *get* here, by *safari?!*

CORA. (*Incensed, storms over to him.*) That does it! I've had enough! You and your kind always did make me sick to my stomach—oh!—sick—to my stomach—it's all coming back—that voice—that marvelous raging voice—

OLIVER. That rage—that marvelously familiar rage—! (*Pries back the foliage from her face.*) Boopsy!

CORA. Snooker-Pie! (*They embrace.*)

J.D. Oliver, what are you doing? You'll miss your boat!

OLIVER. J.D.—you don't understand—this is *she!* My little lady of the gum-wrapper! My long-lost love! I can't go away with Wu Chang *now!*

WU. *Why the hell not?* (OTHERS *all react to this unwonted profanity.*)

OLIVER. Because now I have something at last to *live for!*

J.D. Then—psychologically speaking—this is the moment when you would *least* like to leave this earth?

OLIVER. Why—yes. It would be the rottenest timing imaginable . . . ?

J.D. Then what the hell, Charlie—Let's rub him out the *risky* way! (*Squeals with delight, clapping hands wildly, as*

WU *takes out that .45 and points it Oliverward—though
everybody else except* J.D. *take backsteps of fear, too.*)

OLIVER. J.D.! What is the meaning of this?!

WU. Shut up and stand still, I hate moving targets!

J.D. No, wait, Charlie—don't shoot him yet—not till he
knows *why!* (*Rubs hands together gleefully.*) It will make
revenge all the sweeter!

DEREK. (*A fragile hope, but worth a try.*) Say, listen,
while you're having your little chat— (*Is backing with
SYLVIA toward garden, now, and* GEORGE *and* PEGGY,
sensing his drift, start doing the same.)

GEORGE. (*Picking up the thought.*) —if you don't really
need the *rest* of us any longer—

WU. Hold it right there! (*They all freeze in place.*) That's
better. Now, hurry up, Jenny, this is making me nervous!

CORA. (*Clinging fearfully to* OLIVER.) Making *you*
nervous?! Snooker-Pie, can't you *do* something?

OLIVER. (*Looks incredulously into her face for a
moment; then:*) Such as?! (*Then* ALL *cock an ear hallward
as we hear:*)

SANDERS. (*Off.*) Jane, don't do it, come back here—!

(*We hear two pairs of running feet, and then* JANE *bursts in,
        two paces ahead of* SANDERS; *she stops, distraught,
        flails an arm in the direction of the picture hiding that
        burning fuse, and:*)

JANE. (*Shouts.*) Out! Everybody out! There's a—

SANDERS. (*Grabs her mouth.*) Jane, you'll ruin everything!

JANE. (*Pulls free.*) There's a—

SANDERS. (*Grabs again.*) Jane, we'll lose our jobs!

JANE. (*Pulls free again.*) But there's a—

SANDERS. (*Same business.*) Jane, after all our work, our
hopes, our dreams—!

JANE. (*Same.*) But there's going to be an—

J.D. (*In a rage of frustration, interrupts.*) Jane, will you shut up and let me get on with my vengeance?!

JANE. But you're all going to *die!*

WU. (*Waving gun.*) How did *she* know? She was out in the hall! (*First* SANDERS, *then* JANE, *notice the gun and fling their hands overhead, on:*)

SANDERS. What's going *on* here?

JANE. Yeah, what do you think you're doing?!

WU. If you'd close your *yap* you might find *out!* Little Betsy here is starting to feel mighty heavy, and I've got an itchy trigger-finger, and you and this old geezer are about to buy a one-way ticket to Boot Hill!

J.D. Charlie, what *are* you babbling about?

WU. Search me. That's gangster-talk! (*Levels gun at* OLIVER.) Where do you want it, Mac, in the belly or the back?

J.D. Not *yet,* Charlie, I haven't made my revelatory speech!

WU. And you're not *gonna,* either, shyster!

SANDERS. Is that any way to address a lady?!

WU. (*Shrugs.*) Okay. "*Shysterette!*"

J.D. Charlie—!

WU. Shaddup! And raise your hands like the resta them! (J.D. *does so, wide-eyed with surprise.*) Now listen, Stratton, there's just one way to save your skin: Open that safe, give me the money, and I clear outa here without bloodshed. Deal?

OLIVER. No deal.

CORA. You're so brave!

OLIVER. Nothing of the sort. Without my money, I might as *well* be dead!

JANE. Oh, tell him, sir, please, or he'll kill *all* of us!

GEORGE. Dad, you've got to! Don't get yourself killed! Please!

OLIVER. But how can I survive without my millions?

PEGGY. (*In her practical way.*) Oh, you'll get it back. It's a known fact that remorse eventually floods a thief with regret, and he gives the money back. Of course, it takes a few years, and he does it anonymously, in a plain envelope—

OLIVER. I could *starve* by then! No deal, Wu Chang—or whoever you are.

WU. Then how about I threaten to bump off your *nephew?* What would you say *then,* Stratton?! (OLIVER *considers, turns, looks at a hopefully smiling* DEREK— *whose smile freezes and slowly fades in the thoughtful silence.*)

DEREK. *Uncle Oliver!?*

SYLVIA. Oliver, you can't let him take a shot at Derek—! (DEREK *cravenly sidles behind her, as if she were a protective barrier; she looks down at herself, then up at the barrel of the gun, and adds:*) Especially now.

OLIVER. (*Sighs and relents.*) Ohhhh—I suppose not. He's a pain in the neck, but I can't have him bleeding all over my carpet.

DEREK. Oh, *thank* you, Uncle Oliver . . . I think.

OLIVER. (*To* WU.) The combination is one left, two right, and three left.

SANDERS. As simple as that?!

J.D. Come to think of it, when the safe was installed, Oliver *did* say the combination was easy as one-two-three . . . !

WU. Terrific! Stand back, all of you! (*They shift back from him, always facing him with their hands raised, as he peers about the room.*) Where the hell *is* it?

DEREK. Behind that picture over there.

WU. (*Moves in that direction.*) How do I get to it?

JANE. You may not have to. Any moment now, it may come to *you!*

WU. Come on, come on, back off, everybody! (*As he gets up before picture,* OTHERS *have shifted Downstage, facing him, with their backs to the "fourth wall" of the proscenium, and* WU *with his back to the picture.)* Now—turn around! *(They do, and are now facing us, faces fearful, hands held high over their heads.)* How do I get this picture out of the way? Tell me, quick, or I'm going to start shooting the *women!* One by one, beginning with the *loveliest!* *(*CORA *screams and clutches* OLIVER.*)*

OLIVER. *(Shouts over his shoulder without looking Upstage.)* There's a button on the side of the bookcase, near the bottom corner of the picture. Press that and the picture slides right up.

WU. This isn't a trick—? It doesn't ring an alarm or anything—?

OLIVER. I assure you, it doesn't make a sound. I oil the mechanism once a week, and it is probably the *quietest* secret hiding place in the history of wall safes! There won't even be a squeak!

WU. Well, okay, if I have your word for it—

OLIVER. *Trust* me! You won't hear so much as a whisper! I use plenty of oil.

(And so WU *presses the button, and at this point, of course, the TNT detonates; the effects are all quite simultaneous, but here they are: There is a loud boom of the explosion, the stage BLACKS OUT,* ALL *scream, and then the LIGHTS COME UP immediately, and we see that the picture has slid up to the ceiling, that there is a gaping hole in hitherto-unseen bricks of the wall where the safe had been, lots of smoke boiling out of the hole amid a blizzard of large-denomination bills, and we see* WU *lying face downward, his face on the sofa-cushions, his insteps on the table behind the sofa, and a mound of bills hiding most of him excepting his up-thrust gun-hand, still clutching the weapon. Then the Downstage group all lower their hands, and do not turn around to look Upstage until after we hear:)*

CORA. What *kind* of oil?

(*Now* ALL *turn, see the tableau, and rush to it, doing various things all at once:* PEGGY *rushes to take* WU'S *wrist and feel efficiently for his pulse, while* JANE, SYLVIA *and* CORA *start stuffing money down the front of their dresses, while* GEORGE, DEREK, OLIVER *and* SANDERS *each grab a bottle from the table and proceed to drink directly from the neck of it, and* J.D. *deftly takes the gun from* WU'S *limp fingers.* OLIVER *sees this, and:*)

OLIVER. Good work, J.D.! Keep him covered in case he starts to dig his way *out!*

DEREK. (*Setting bottle aside—as do the other men.*) He'll never get past *me*—digging *my* way *in!* (*Starts burrowing across table into pile of money.*)

OLIVER. *Control* yourselves, *all* of you! (*Everybody pauses where they are, and he notes:*) J.D.—why do you have that odd look on your face? Why are you pointing that gun at me?

PEGGY. (*Gasps, drops* WU'S *wrist.*) Oliver! I just remembered! *She* was the one who put Wu Chang *up* to this!

ALL OTHERS BUT J.D. AND WU. (*In rhythmic unison.*) Good grief! That's right! (*They all raise their hands.*)

OLIVER. Before you shoot—*why,* J.D., *why?*

J.D. All right. I'll tell you. And then you all die. First Oliver, then all the rest of you, one by one!

PEGGY. You'll never get away with it!

J.D. And why not?

PEGGY. (*Ever the lecturer.*) Your conscience will give you no peace. I have read many clinical records of criminal psychology, and it is common knowledge that the onset of remorse soon deprives a murderess of all happiness, until all the pleasures of life become meaningless ashes, and she realizes it was the wrong thing to do, after all, and repents.

SYLVIA. That'll be consoling when they bury us.

J.D. Enough talk! Oliver Stratton—say your prayers!

DEREK. (*Leans over to touch* OLIVER's *sleeve.*) *Long* prayers!

SYLVIA. (*Remember, now, she has worn those dark glasses since Act Two.*) Wait! Before all the shooting starts, let me have one last look at all that beautiful money! (*Removes glasses.*) Oh my! It's all so nice and—and— negotiable! (*Starts to sob, but stops on:*)

J.D. (*Takes back-step.*) *Wolfgang!*

OTHERS. What?

J.D. That eye—that black ring around it—it—it's just like the one on my beloved schnauzer! (*Starts to lower gun.*) I can't go through with it! It's like a sign from heaven—as though Wolfgang had come back to tell me, "No! Don't! It wasn't really Oliver's fault!"

OLIVER. *What* wasn't my fault? (*He and* OTHERS *will slowly lower hands, during:*)

J.D. When my schnauzer died, it was killed by a milk-truck—one of the *Stratton* milktrucks! My little ball of beloved frisky fur—in a cold grave, just because Oliver kept those damned bottles rolling down the road, so a lot of people could gorge on Rice Krispies! I vowed revenge! I got this job as your lawyer, hired Charlie to play Wu Chang, showed you that phony ad I'd put in the New York Times, worked on your loneliness for your lost love to make you want to become a monk—everything! But now— (*Gun finally hangs limply at her side.*) looking at Miss Crane's black-eyed face, I am reminded of poor Wolfgang's gentle nature, his natural sweetness, his cuddliness—he would not have wanted me to do this sort of thing—and yet—what other sort of revenge *is* there?

SYLVIA. (*Swiftly.*) You could always give up drinking milk—?!

PEGGY. Nonsense! As the dairy farmer commercials always tell us, "You *never* outgrow your need for milk!" (*Lectures again, as fellow-menacees stare at her.*) Yes, leading medical authorities agree that milk is the one essential food. It gives people strong bones, white teeth—

SYLVIA. And *shattered skulls*, if you don't shut up!

J.D. (*Wavering, uncertain.*) Do you think—do you really think—giving up milk would be enough?

GEORGE. It's certainly worth a try!

JANE. There are *other* things to drink!

SANDERS. *Plenty* of other things!

OLIVER. Coffee—!

DEREK. Tea—!

SYLVIA. Gin—bourbon—scotch—rum—vodka—brandy—tequila—!

CORA. (*Studying her, narrow-eyed.*) Are you *sure* you're not Miss Brent?

OLIVER. (*Moves gently to* J.D., *takes gun.*) J.D. . . . Jenny . . . I didn't know. You should have told me. But I am going to make it up to you. I shall build a statue of Wolfgang, an exact replica of your beloved schnauzer, in solid gold, with ruby eyes and a platinum collar—a *life-sized* statue!

DEREK. (Sotto voce *"aside" to* GEORGE.) Good thing Wolfgang wasn't an *elephant!*

J.D. A statue, Oliver? That's—that's awfully good of you, but—where would you put it?

OLIVER. In a place of honor—a place it deserves—right out in front of my dairy, on a marble pedestal, with a suitable inscription—!

J.D. (*Almost weeping with happiness.*) What inscription?

GEORGE. (*As* OLIVER *flounders, jumps into the breach.*) "Wolfgang the Schnauzer—he got a raw deal!"

SYLVIA. (*Lurching into the act, as it were.*) "You're playing with fire when you meet a big wheel!"

OLIVER. (*Glares at her, says crisply:*) We can *skip* that *last* bit!

SYLVIA. Sorry, just trying to help . . . ! (*Reacts as* WU *groans and starts stirring under bills.*) Oh, look, everyone, here comes the world's wealthiest groundhog!

WU. (*After being helped out from under money onto his feet.*) Wow! I'm lucky it wasn't in *singles!*

J.D. Oh, Oliver—what are you going to do—about me and Charlie, I mean?

OLIVER. Well—I *should* inform the police, I suppose, but—I think you've both learned your lesson. Besides, I've found my long-lost love, and I'm too happy to prosecute anybody!

J.D. (*All choked up.*) You marvelous man! I—I don't know what I've done to deserve a friend like you! (*Exits weeping to hall.*)

WU. (*Disgusted, calls after her:*) You were probably rotten to your mother! (*Exits to hall.*)

(*Over next few lines, everyone will pair off as they speak—*
GEORGE/PEGGY, DEREK/SYLVIA, OLIVER/CORA,
SANDERS/JANE, *Downstage of the sofa.* JANE *and*
SANDERS *start for hall.*)

JANE. Herbert, you owe me a dollar-fifty for that stick of TNT.

SANDERS. Ninety-eight cents. You bought it at a Macy's sale.

JANE. You would remember that. (*They exit.*)

DEREK. (*Picks up fallen paper from wherever he left it.*) Well, I guess I may as well tear up my ticket to financial security, now that Oliver's back, with no intention of heading for Tibet . . . (*Peers curiously at it.*) What the devil is "W.L.D.D."?

CORA. Why—that's the Women's League for Dry Distilleries.

SYLVIA. (*Snatches paper from* DEREK, *reads it.*) Oh, no! Derek, you dope—you didn't take the will—you took the pledge!

DEREK. (*Groans, moves toward table.*) I need a drink!

GEORGE. You should have thought of that before you signed the paper.

CORA. Fight the urge, Derek! Don't dabble in the devil's brew!

SYLVIA. Honey, have you ever tried it?

CORA. Tried it? I was *weaned* on it!

PEGGY. Then why do you preach against it?

CORA. A job's a job. I don't *practice* what I preach.

OLIVER. Cora, my darling, listen—lest I lose you again, I am going to say something—three little words that will make our lives complete, that will fill you with peace and happiness. Do you know what those three little words are?

CORA. (*Nods.*) "Quit your job!"

OLIVER. No. "Let's go eat!" . . . Come on, there's still a lot of dinner left!

PEGGY. (*Hurrying after him and* CORA *as they exit.*) Now, Oliver, you *know* what garlic does to your insides—!

GEORGE. (*Hurrying after her.*) Peggy, don't you *ever* go *off duty?!*

PEGGY. (*Turns to him.*) Nursing is a sacred trust. After all, your father's stomach is in my hands! (*Exits to hall.*)

GEORGE. (*Looks back toward* DEREK *and* SYLVIA, *smiles shyly.*) She's pretty disgusting, but she's mine, all mine! (*Exits.*)

DEREK. (*Moves wearily to sofa, where he will shove some bills aside and sit,* SYLVIA *sitting beside him.*) Well— here we are, poor again!

SYLVIA. It's like a nightmare—a permanent mental breakdown. When I think of our future—the Automat— those long train rides out here—tossing pebbles at your window—! I can't stand it! I can't! (*Sags wearily against him, her cheek upon his shoulder.*)

DEREK. I understand the living is cheaper in Brazil, if we could only get there.

SYLVIA. How well can you swim?

DEREK. I never had time to learn—I was too busy learning to scrounge.

SYLVIA. And even *that* you don't do very successfully!

DEREK. I know, I know. Ah, darling, darling, what are we going to do? You certainly can't support *me*, and I'm too klutzy to get *any* kind of work! If only Oliver would lay an endowment on me, or—or— (*Has been idly fingering some bills, suddenly realizes what they are, and sits up, his mouth gaping.*) Sylvia—look! Look what we're sitting on!

SYLVIA. (*Realizes, grabs up handful, stares at it, then at him.*) Oh, Derek—do we dare?!

DEREK. (*Stands, staring down at money.*) I wonder— there's no *extradition* from Brazil—but could we *get* there before the police caught up to us?

SYLVIA. Well—these are mostly all hundred-dollar bills—we could take a *few* handfuls—they might not be missed—you know, just enough for our boat-fare—and the bills I stuffed into my dress might be enough to set us up in a little house near a banana plantation, maybe—I mean—no one would ever know—

DEREK. (*Lifts fistful of bills, tentatively.*) You know—it's not *often* people take ocean voyages—we wouldn't *have* to go third class—not on a one-time deal . . . I mean—it's going to be a sort of honeymoon, so why not do it first-class? (*Pockets the fistful of bills.*)

SYLVIA. (*Ominously.*) A *sort* of honeymoon, Derek—?!

DEREK. Oh, we could legalize it in Maryland, en route, I suppose—but that would mean tipping the Justice of the Peace . . . (*Pockets another fistful.*)

SYLVIA. Oh, and of course, there's the cost of the ring—! (*Stuffs another fistful down the front of her dress.*)

[*NOTE: the following dialogue accelerates faster and faster, each line followed by the grabbing-and-stuffing of a handful of bills, then larger handfuls, then both handfuls, faster and stuffinger and wildly happier, as the CURTAIN STARTS SLOWLY DOWNWARD—*]

DEREK. I suppose I should wear a tux—
SYLVIA. We need someone to sing ''Oh Promise Me''—
DEREK. And a dozen roses for our stateroom—

SYLVIA. Two dozen—ten dozen—a dozen dozen—!

DEREK. And if we have a child, he'll need shoes—!

SYLVIA. Socks—trousers—lunch money—!

DEREK. And papering the nursery when the other kids come along—!

SYLVIA. And extra rooms on the house—!

DEREK. And all those bicycles—!

SYLVIA. And the bare essentials of life, like bread—!

DEREK. And fresh fruit—!

SYLVIA. And a mink coat—!

DEREK. Champagne—caviar—!

SYLVIA. Caviar—champagne—!

BOTH. More caviar! More champagne! More! More! More! (*And they are still ad-libbing "More!" and stuffing and laughing and reeling with delight, as—*)

The Curtain Falls

PROPERTY LIST

ACT ONE, Scene 1:

Preset: vases of flowers at ends of table, tray with bottled liquor, siphon, glasses, ice, etc., at center of table; SYLVIA's purse on desk; supply of paper, pencils and pens in center desk drawer

J.D.: topcoat to be carried on at first entrance

JANE: featherduster

Scene 2: (see RECOMMENDATIONS for setup)

JANE: pitcher of water at top of act; tray of "baked alaskas" [only WU's need be edible], plates and forks from kitchen; tray of soup from kitchen [only the one she uses need be edible] with spoons

SYLVIA: large dark sunglasses with makeup "shiner" beneath

DEREK: pitcher of "gin" [water will do] from library, twice

DEREK/SYLVIA/PEGGY: sandwiches from kitchen [edible]

ACT TWO, Scene 1:

Reset: "dinner table" back behind sofa, place liquor, flowers, etc. back atop it as at top of Act One, but SYLVIA's purse [which had been on table before "creation of dining room" (see RECOMMENDATIONS) should now be cleared from stage]

SANDERS: toolbox containing hammer and chisel; later, electric drill with dangling cord; later, manual bug-spray gun from garden; later, toolbox from garden

Scene 2:

Preset: those scribbled "scripts" in the hands of the four conspirators; MOST IMPORTANT: at this time, make *sure* liquor tray is set to one side of the table, and *not* in the center anymore, because there *must* be a clear center space for WU to get into position across table and sofa for the post-explosion tableau in Act Three,

110

and now is the only logical time [the remainder of action in the play being practically continuous] for that placement to be made

CORA: hat, boa, and umbrella, plus armload of pamphlets and papers under her non-umbrella-toting arm

ACT THREE:

Preset: pamphlets and papers on desktop; make sure plenty of liquor left in bottles for heavy drinking that takes place in this act

CORA: umbrella in hand at top of act, but she may leave it offstage forever after her first exit

WU: easily accessible .45 automatic inside robe

GEORGE/PEGGY/SYLVIA/DEREK: be sure they remember to bring back bottle and glasses from garden after their exit with them, and *not* to leave them anywhere but on off-center tray, for WU's safety during explosion

SANDERS: roll of tape and stick of TNT with fuse, in pocket

JANE: wooden match (with spares, in case of mis-strike) in pocket of maid's uniform

(for CORA's cumulative dishevelment, see RECOMMENDATIONS)

Set *during* act: "explosion"-effect items (see RECOMMENDATIONS)

SOUND EFFECTS

"Punch" when DEREK decks SYLVIA (have him near-miss while she snaps head aside as if from blow, while simultaneously some offstage player *claps hands* once, sharply, at instant of "blow"—effect will be startlingly real, as if he'd really struck her); CRASH of kitchenware via "Mildred," plus her FOOTFALLS and SLAM of door as she leaves; CLAPPING offstage from SANDERS when asked to "give a hand"; EXPLOSION, which should be the type that starts with a roaring *blam*, followed by fast-dying *rumbles*.

RECOMMENDATIONS

1) Since it's much easier to work when one can see what one is doing, the set-change between the scenes in Act One can be better—and more amusingly—accomplished if you, rather than have a blackout, convert to strobe-lighting of the stage, for that early-silent-movie effect, simultaneously turning on some Frantic Piano Music over the sound system, and allow the performers themselves to flip over that tabletop [it's not as though the new "set" is actually going to *fool* the audience as to what it is], arrange the chairs, drop the backing-curtain (or slide backing-screens into place, or even—if you like—simply turning off all *lighting* of the upstage area, since audiences enjoy "going along with" the imaginary locales of a play), place the drinking-glasses, etc., and then get into position for the start of the second scene, at which time the strobe-light halts, and the play progresses. This is not only a more efficient way of handling the change, but it also serves to keep the action going (a lull in a comedy is the deadliest of sins) for the audience, and as a bonus to the cast, you will find that the audience will applaud the scene-shifters' efforts as the music stops.

(NOTE: SYLVIA's "shiner" can be applied to her eye during JANE's speech to "Mildred" at the start of Scene 2, before she and DEREK enter dining room.)

2) For CORA's various re-entrances from the garden in Act Three, you will of course not *really* jam the poor lady's straw hat down about her throat, or rend her pamphlet nightly, but simply have a separate matching hat already rent, and a pair of matching pamphlet halves for her to carry on. And if the "gagging" with the boa renders it too soggy for re-use, then have a duplicate boa, too, for *that* manifestation. The twigs, finally, should be carefully wired into an actual costume-over-the-costume that she can wear onstage

112

with no fear of its tumbling off and cluttering the stage; the face-covering part should be designed so that she can see her way about, but remain unrecognizable till OLIVER exposes her face to his adoring view.

3) The TNT explosion: This is handled very simply, by means of having a pre-recorded explosion which is sounded *precisely* as the blackout occurs (a fraction before or after hurts the effect), and during that extremely short interval of darkness, here is what happens: You will have *already* (the moment the picture is lowered to hide the burning fuse) had the stage crew remove the pre-cut jagged-wall segment on which is mounted the fake safe-front [the safe is never actually opened, so a non-functioning door on it will suffice for the show], then have stacked packets of dusty "money" *leaning against* the back of the picture, and then placed a "brick" backdrop upstage of this; you will also have, overhead in the flies above the sofa-and-table area, a container with a large number—at least three bushels—of loose "bills" and more "plaster dust" awaiting the blackout-and-explosion cue. Most important: During that brief interval of darkness, your WU CHANG must hasten downstage and slide belly-down across table and sofa into position to be beneath the falling blizzard of bills and dust; it is the length of time it takes your player to get into this position that determines the time of the blackout, of course. [The sound of the "explosion" plus the screams of the downstage players will cover any noise WU CHANG may make at this juncture.] The effect the audience sees, of course, will be: Blackout—explosion and scream—return of lights—and a view of dust, cascading packets of money from the gaping hole in the wall, and a rain of bills and dust still coming downward (as if blown ceiling-high by the blast) over the would-be robber, WU CHANG. If timed right, this will get gratifying applause and laughter from the audience, and hold them merrily in your debt for the remainder of the play.

SCENE DESIGN
A TURN FOR THE NURSE

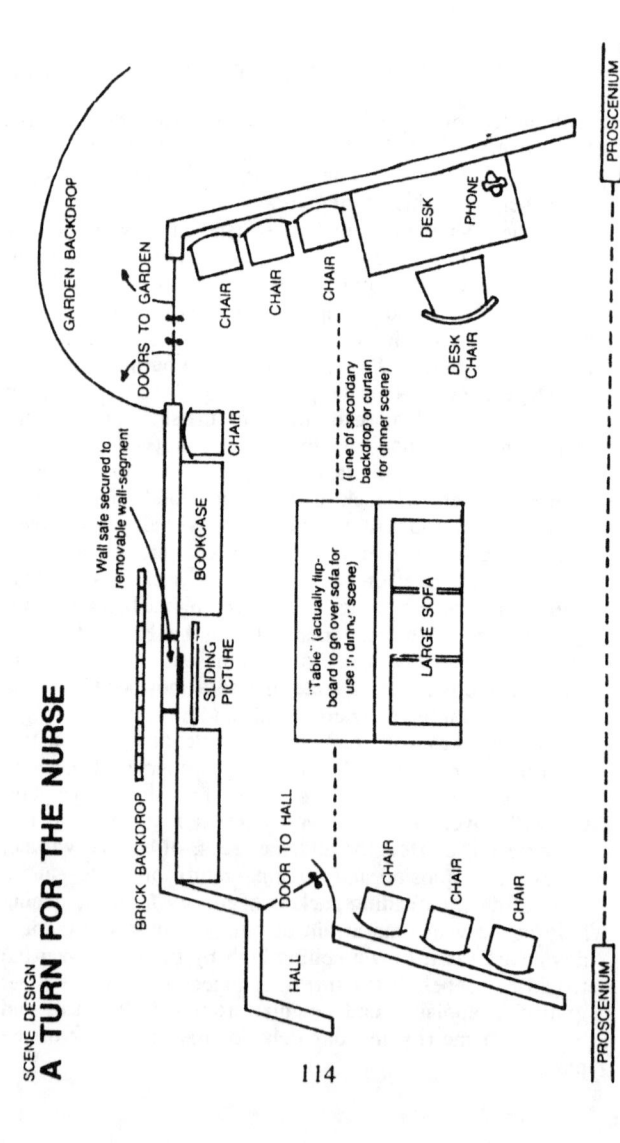

114

MUSIC USE NOTE

Licensees are solely responsible for obtaining formal written permission from copyright owners to use copyrighted music in the performance of this play and are strongly cautioned to do so. If no such permission is obtained by the licensee, then the licensee must use only original music that the licensee owns and controls. Licensees are solely responsible and liable for all music clearances and shall indemnify the copyright owners of the play(s) and their licensing agent, Samuel French, against any costs, expenses, losses and liabilities arising from the use of music by licensees. Please contact the appropriate music licensing authority in your territory for the rights to any incidental music.

IMPORTANT BILLING AND CREDIT REQUIREMENTS

If you have obtained performance rights to this title, please refer to your licensing agreement for important billing and credit requirements.